Morgan Family Medics

Saving lives…and hearts!

Meet pediatric heart surgeon Anthony Morgan and his estranged son, paramedic Jonno Morgan, who is no stranger to living life on the edge. But for these two men, their lives will never be the same when nurse Elsie and trainee paramedic Brie enter their worlds.

Secret Son to Change His Life

Seven years ago, Brie's dreams came true when she spent one fun night with Jonno before he was due to leave. And then her life was rocked when she discovered she was pregnant, and her son had spina bifida. Now Jonno's back and she can finally reveal the secret she's been longing to tell him…

How to Rescue the Heart Doctor

When Anthony Morgan's relationship with his son broke down, he felt the hole in his life would never be replaced. Until nurse Elsie walks into his operating room! But she is the protective mother of Brie and grandmother to his newly discovered grandson. Will finding each other lead to the second chance they never thought they would have?

Don't miss this hugely emotional generational duet where happy families are made!

Both books are available now from Harlequin Medical Romance

Dear Reader,

Links between characters are the foundation of any story, but it's a bonus for me when I can both read and write links that span more than one book. I love that I can not only follow other people I've met into their own stories, but I get glimpses of what's happening to the people I already know and love.

I'm also excited about exploring a totally new link in the second book of this duo, an intergenerational one, with Anthony and Elsie's story being my first romance between an older couple. I know from experience that being older is no barrier to falling in love and finding happiness. It can, in fact, be even more special.

This duo may be centered on fathers and sons, but it's the women in these two books—Brie and her mother, Elsie—who are the catalysts for these stories, and I hope you love them as much as I do.

Happy reading,

Alison xxx

SECRET SON
TO CHANGE HIS LIFE

———

ALISON ROBERTS

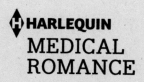

HARLEQUIN

MEDICAL
ROMANCE

♦ HARLEQUIN®
MEDICAL
ROMANCE™

Recycling programs
for this product may
not exist in your area.

ISBN-13: 978-1-335-73768-7

Secret Son to Change His Life

Copyright © 2023 by Alison Roberts

For questions and comments about the quality of this book,
please contact us at CustomerService@Harlequin.com.

Harlequin Enterprises ULC
22 Adelaide St. West, 41st Floor
Toronto, Ontario M5H 4E3, Canada
www.Harlequin.com

Printed in U.S.A.

Alison Roberts has been lucky enough to live in the South of France for several years recently but is now back in her home country of New Zealand. She is also lucky enough to write for the Harlequin Medical Romance line. A primary school teacher in a former life, she later became a qualified paramedic. She loves to travel and dance, drink champagne, and spend time with her daughter and her friends. **Alison Roberts** is the author of over one hundred books!

Books by Alison Roberts

Harlequin Medical Romance

Two Tails Animal Refuge

The Vet's Unexpected Family

Royal Christmas at Seattle General

Falling for the Secret Prince

Stolen Nights with the Single Dad
Christmas Miracle at the Castle
Miracle Baby, Miracle Family
A Paramedic to Change Her Life
One Weekend in Prague
The Doctor's Christmas Homecoming

Visit the Author Profile page
at Harlequin.com for more titles.

**Praise for
Alison Roberts**

"Ms. Roberts has delivered a delightful read in this book where the chemistry between this couple was strong from the moment they meet...[and] the romance was heart-warming."

—*Harlequin Junkie* on
Melting the Trauma Doc's Heart

CHAPTER ONE

THE ADDRESS WAS in an ordinary street, in an ordinary suburb towards the northern side of Bristol, a three-bedroom, end-of-terrace house not dissimilar to the one Brianna Henderson lived in herself.

As she pushed open the gate to the straight, narrow concrete path that led towards the front door with its honour guard of tidy rose bushes on either side, there was nothing to suggest something very *un*ordinary was happening inside this house.

Nothing to warn her that a split second could change *everything...*

This felt more like a dream come true, in fact. This was Brie's first callout, on her first official shift as a newly qualified paramedic—the achievement of a dream that could so easily have been seen as completely dead in the water not that long ago.

Okay, so maybe it was only an activation

of a personal medical alarm—the kind that so many elderly, frail or disabled people could use to summon assistance. Her senior crew partner, Simon, had actually rolled his eyes when the call came through.

'Don't get too excited,' he'd warned. 'Bet you they've pressed the button on their pendant by accident. Either that or they've fallen out of their chair and need some help to get up off the floor.'

'But don't they usually contact family members or neighbours first unless there's something really wrong? This is a priority call.' Brie was already several steps ahead of Simon now. The vehicle they were heading for was parked in the garage at the back of one of Bristol's largest ambulance stations.

'They will have forgotten to put their hearing aids in so they won't have heard anyone calling through the loudspeaker to find out what's going on.'

'What about the banging noises they could hear? And the scream?'

'I bet the telly's on in another room. Really loud because of the no hearing aids.' But it must have been very clear to Simon that Brie was not about to dismiss this call as a waste of time and resources. 'You can drive,' he'd told her with a smile. 'It's a good chance for you to play with all the bells and whistles.'

Apparently it was also a good chance for Brie to take the lead in assessing the situation and she took a big breath as she climbed the couple of steps at the end of the path and knocked on the door that was slightly ajar.

'Ambulance,' she called as she pushed the door open. 'Hello...? Where are you?'

Simon was right behind her, the handle of the defibrillator in one hand and an oxygen cylinder in the other. This might turn out to be a false alarm but protocol made it necessary to carry whatever they might need if they found themselves faced with something as serious as a cardiac arrest.

The silence that met Brie's call was the first sign that something wasn't quite right. Someone who was alone and waiting for help would always answer that call if they were able to. If they weren't alone, there would probably have been someone waiting at the door, or the gate, to direct them to where they were needed. Or was the explanation simply that someone couldn't hear the call because they had forgotten to put their hearing aids in?

They were in a small hallway that had a staircase leading upstairs to where bedrooms and a bathroom would most likely be. Brie assumed that the door ahead of them on the right would lead to a living room and kitchen dining area, like her own house and, given the time of day, it was more likely that the elderly or disabled occupant of the house would be downstairs. With a glance over her shoulder to confirm that Simon agreed with her choice, she walked forward, knocking on the interior door again before pushing it open.

'Ambulance,' she called again. She didn't want to give an elderly person a horrible fright by barging in without any warning. 'Is anybody here?'

It only took that split second, after stepping into the room, to capture what she could see but it took another beat of time to process something so unexpected.

An elderly woman was sitting, bolt up-right, on a couch in front of the bay window that faced the street. Brie could see the ambulance she'd been driving less than a minute ago, parked on the road outside. She had turned the siren off well before turning into this suburban street but the blue lights were still flashing on the roof.

The woman looked terrified and she was clutching her chest as if she was in the kind of pain a heart attack could cause but she

wasn't looking back at Brie. She was staring straight in front of her to where a much
younger woman was being strangled. Her
face was bright red and her eyes were bulging
as she clawed desperately at the two hands
around her neck. The man who was doing
the strangling was the only person looking
at Brie and she'd never seen such a look of
sheer rage.

Training told her she needed to get out of
there as fast as possible. Her own and her
crew's safety was paramount because if they
got hurt they wouldn't be able to do their job
and help anyone. But Simon was right behind
her, blocking the door, and he was still taking
in what he was seeing in what seemed like a
frozen scene in front of them.

Suddenly, it wasn't frozen. The younger
woman crumpled and fell to the floor as the
man let go of her neck and shoved her away
with a vehement curse. The elderly woman
on the couch cried out in fear as he began
moving but he was heading straight for Brie,
who instinctively stepped out of his path. Her
training in self-defence was kicking in and
she slipped the backpack off her shoulders
and held it in front of her as she moved, ready
to use it by throwing it at the man or as a barrier in case of a knife attack.

But it seemed that the angry man was more intent on escaping the room and he rushed to the door, pushing Simon out of the way with such force that the senior paramedic's feet almost left the floor as he hurtled backwards. Brie could actually hear Simon's head strike the wooden edge of the staircase with a sickening crunch.

It was Brie's turn to freeze for another moment. The crumpled woman on the floor was moving, pushing herself up to a sitting position. The woman on the couch was crying and still clutching her chest. It was the groan from Simon outside the door that had to take priority, however. She found him sitting, holding his head, his eyes shut.

'Call for backup,' he told Brie. 'And get out of here.'

'I'm not leaving you,' she said, dismayed to hear her voice shake.

'He might…come back…'

Brie swallowed hard, her mind racing. Having her own life in potentially immediate danger on her very first shift was the last thing she'd expected. How would her mother cope if the worst happened? How on earth had she thought that following the dream of this career had been a good idea? Back in the days when she'd been working as a triple nine call taker and dispatcher for the ambulance service, she'd always been so frustrated by trying to assist with critical situations from the other end of a telephone line. Coaching people to provide CPR or, ironically, advising them to try and find a safe space if they were in a situation where their own lives could be in danger. She'd never forgive herself if chasing that dream of doing what she'd wanted to do so much—being the person who took over when the telephone contact was no longer needed—ended up ruining the lives of the people she loved the most. Her mum. And her son...

But she'd never forgive herself if she ran away from people who needed help either. Brie knew she had no choice, but she did have to think fast and the first thing she needed to do was to try and prevent the situation getting any worse. She slammed the front door shut and locked it. She'd check the back door next but, first, she had to get backup on the way. She reached for the radio clipped to her shoulder and pressed the button to transmit her voice, which wasn't shaking nearly so much now.

'Unit Four-Zero-Three to Control,' she said clearly. 'Code Black. I repeat... Code Black.'

A code she'd never dreamed of having to

use. One that would alert any emergency vehicles nearby that assistance was urgently needed for a situation that was dangerous enough to be a threat to life.

'Roger that, Four-Zero-Three.'

'It's a violent assault,' Brie added as she crouched beside Simon. 'At least two victims. Paramedic down. Attacker still in the area.'

'Roger that, Four-Zero-Three. Standby... We've got assistance on the way.'

Simon was trying to get up but fell back with another groan. 'Too...dizzy...' he said.

'Don't move,' Brie ordered. 'I'll be right back. I've got to check on the others and make sure the back door's locked.'

Fear for her own safety had evaporated as an adrenaline rush galvanised Brie. She raced back into the living room. The older woman hadn't moved from the couch and still looked terrified.

'Is he gone?' The words wobbled. 'Really... gone?'

'I've locked the front door,' Brie assured her. 'Help's on its way. I'm going to check the back door now. Who was he—do you know?'

'My husband...'

It was the younger woman on the floor who spoke, as Brie moved past her into the kitchen. Her voice was croaky and Brie could hear a whistling sound as she grabbed a breath after speaking. How much damage had that near strangulation caused? Was she in danger of losing an airway that was only just patent?

Brie could see that the back door of the house was ajar and then, to her horror, she caught the ominous shape, in her peripheral vision, of someone moving fast down the side path through the kitchen window. With shaking hands, she pushed the door shut and heard the snib lock catch just as the handle got rattled. A volley of swear words followed.

'I'll get you!' the man shouted, banging on the door. 'Just you wait...'

The pane of glass in the top of the door shattered and Brie pressed her hand to her mouth, waiting for the hand to reach in to undo the lock. Instead there was more profanity from outside.

'I've *cut* myself... This is all your fault...'

Brie held her breath. In a sudden silence outside she could hear the sound of a siren, which could well be the first available unit responding to her Code Black. She hoped it would be the police responding first. With a violent offender still present, the scene would have to be secured before any other medics could be allowed in and she needed help as fast as possible. Simon was out of action, the elderly woman on the couch might have chest pain that could indicate something serious like a heart attack, but the younger woman who'd been attacked was in respiratory distress so she needed the most urgent care. It was the top of the list in the ABC of assessment. Airway, Breathing and Circulation.

The high-pitched whistling sounds of obstructed breathing were even louder as Brie dropped to her knees beside the woman, who was now sitting and leaning forward—another sign of respiratory distress.

'My name's Brie,' she said. She unzipped the pack she'd carried in and then opened a pouch inside it. 'I'm going to put a mask on you and get some oxygen on, okay?'

As she picked up the oxygen cylinder that was lying by the door where Simon had dropped it, Brie could see that her crew partner was still holding his head in his hands.

'I'm okay,' he told her. 'But if I try and move I'm going to throw up.'

'I heard a siren,' Brie said. 'Backup's not far away.'

The woman on the couch was watching what she was doing. 'Her name's Carla,' she said. 'She's my daughter. She came here to try and get away from her husband. I didn't know what to do… That's why I pushed my button…when he wasn't looking…'

'You did exactly the right thing,' Brie said. She pulled a plastic mask from its packaging and unfurled the tubing to attach to the oxygen cylinder. She had the mask in one hand and the elastic to pull over Carla's head in the other but, even before she could get the mask near her patient's face, Carla's head slumped as she lost consciousness and she toppled sideways.

In the same moment, she heard glass being broken again in the kitchen and then the unmistakable sound of a door opening. Brie could feel her heart actually stop for a split second as she looked up, but the first impression of the uniform this man was wearing was enough to reassure her that this wasn't Carla's violent husband back for another go. It was, unexpectedly, a critical care paramedic—part of an elite squad that worked alone, as part of an air ambulance service or a general station like the one Brie had been fortunate enough to get a position at. The critical care paramedics had well-equipped vehicles with gear and skills that enabled them to respond to major, life-threatening events to provide the highest level of pre-hospital care.

It was the best backup that Brie could have

hoped for but that didn't stop her heart skipping another beat as she saw the man's face clearly for the first time.

It *couldn't* be…could it?

Jonno?

The man who'd changed her entire life in the space of a single night?

The last man she'd thought she would ever see again?

'What's happened?'

The query was crisp but he wasn't looking at Brie. He'd dropped to his knees beside Carla and he gripped and shook her shoulder. She didn't have time to answer him before he spoke again, but she still wasn't the focus of his attention.

'Can you hear me?' he asked Carla loudly. 'Can you open your eyes for me?'

Getting no response, he tipped Carla's head back to open her airway and then touched the red marks on her neck to assess any injuries and find her pulse, focusing on what he could see and hear of her breathing at the same time. He slid a rapid sideways glance in Brie's direction.

'So what's happened? I was just round the corner when the Code Black alert came through.'

'Attempted strangulation,' Brie responded.

Did he recognise her voice? Was that why he fired that sharp glance at her face? Brie was desperately trying to bury her own recognition of this man and not only the visceral response her body was generating but what the potential repercussions in her own life could be. She couldn't let herself go there. Not yet.

'She was conscious and talking but the stridor got worse,' she added quickly. 'And...she just lost consciousness a few seconds ago.'

'Grab a bag mask for me, would you?' His gaze was back on their patient and his voice was calm. 'I need both an oral and nasal airway as well, and how 'bout cranking that oxygen up to full tilt. Fifteen litres.'

He looked over his shoulder to where Carla's mother was staring at him. Brie saw him frown as she handed him the curved plastic oral airway, the soft rubber tube that was the nasopharyngeal airway and the mask with the ventilation bag and a soft reservoir bag attached. He slipped the devices intended to keep airways open into place and then snapped open the compressed ventilation bag, taking another concerned glance at Carla's mother.

'Have you got chest pain?' he asked.

She nodded.

'Have you had it before? Do you get angina?'

She nodded again.

'Is this pain the same as normal?'

'Yes... Should I use my spray, do you think? It's in my pocket.'

'Yes, please do.'

Jonno smiled at the elderly woman and if Brie had been in any doubt that this was the man she remembered all too well it vanished in that moment. She'd spoken to Jonathon Morgan via radio transmission for years when she'd worked in the control room. More than long enough to hear about the charismatic paramedic's exploits and develop rather a serious crush on him, but it wasn't until she'd met him at that party and he'd smiled at her—just like that—that she'd really fallen for him. Hook, line and sinker. Head over heels. A brief fantasy that had been fulfilled beyond her wildest dreams. For one night. Because that had been the first and last time Brie had seen Jonno. Nearly seven years ago now.

'We'll look after you just as soon as we can,' Jonno told Carla's mother.

Then he looked back at Brie and she saw the flash in his eyes that was the moment he had definitely recognised *her*. Not that he was going to acknowledge it in any way. He

knew better than she did that this was most
definitely not the place or the time and, to his
credit, Jonno was ultimately professional. He
didn't miss a beat in his focus on what was
going on around them.

'Are you working alone?' he asked.

'No—my partner, Simon, got attacked.
He's in the hallway. Conscious, but he's had
a hard knock to his head and he's too dizzy
to move.'

As if to back up her explanation and add to
the feeling of chaos, they could hear a groan
from Simon and then the sound of him being
sick.

'The guy that attacked him might still be
around,' Brie warned. 'That's why I called a
Code Black. He tried to break in through the
back door just before you arrived.'

Jonno's eyebrows rose a fraction and Brie
could almost see him processing all the im-
plications and assigning priorities. There was
a frisson of something like respect in there
as well. Because she hadn't run away from
a terrifying situation herself? Or did he realise how huge a fright he must have given
her by breaking in through the back door the
way he had?

'The police won't be far away,' he said.
'Don't worry about what might or might not

be going on outside. It could mean that we'll have to work by ourselves in here for a while, though, until they get the scene secured. You okay with that?'

Brie nodded but she bit her lip. 'I'm just glad you're here,' she murmured.

'Same.' Jonno raised his voice. 'Simon? Can you hear me?'

'Yeah…'

'Hang in there, mate. We'll come and have a look at you in a sec.' He lowered his voice to speak to Brie again. 'He's conscious and talking so he has a patent airway. Our first priority has to be here.' He squeezed the bag he was holding to pump more oxygen into Carla's lungs. 'Those marks on her neck suggest some soft tissue injury that could start causing enough swelling to close her airway.' He shifted his glance to where the life-pack Simon had been carrying had been abandoned by the door. 'Can you get a pulse oximeter on and some ECG dots? A blood pressure would be good too. I'm going to get IV access and I think we'll be looking at intubation sooner rather than later.'

Taking basic vital signs was something Brie was more than confident to do. She stuck the sticky dots for monitoring Carla's heart into place and clipped the oxygen saturation probe onto her finger while the trace on the screen settled. Then she wrapped the blood pressure cuff around one arm and pushed the button for an automatic reading to be done. Jonno was unrolling pouches from his own kit between delivering puffs of oxygen to Carla and Brie felt a beat of nervousness as she saw the instruments and drugs that it would be years before she could become qualified to use. Was she even capable of being a useful assistant with something as invasive as intubating a patient?

Maybe Jonno could see those nerves as he glanced up because his gaze was reassuring and his tone still perfectly calm.

'Can I get you to come and take over the bagging while I get IV access, please, Brie?'

The subtext to his request was just as clear.

We've got this. I know you're scared but it's okay... I'll talk you through anything you need to do...

And...he'd remembered her name. Brie scrambled to kneel above Carla's head, holding the mask firmly over her mouth and nose with one hand to make sure the air couldn't leak out and squeezing the thick plastic of the bag with her other hand to force the oxygen in.

But...wow... There was a tingling sensation in Brie's body that was impossible to ignore. After so many years and having only really met her on that one occasion, Jonno remembered her name. Did he remember anything else about that night? With something like desperation, Brie shoved the memories that were so keen to surface aside. She knew that they had the potential to be overwhelming.

Not now, she told herself. *Please...not now...*

Jonno was working swiftly and smoothly, sliding a cannula into a vein in Carla's arm and attaching it to a bag of saline. He was keeping a close eye on the numbers the screen of the defibrillator was displaying and Brie could see that it wasn't looking good. The heart rate was increasing steadily and the level of circulating oxygen was dropping. What they were already doing to try and keep Carla's airway open and her breathing adequate was clearly not working well enough.

If Jonno could hear the more than one approaching siren outside that Brie was aware of, he didn't acknowledge them. Instead, he looked completely focused on what was directly in front of him as he caught Brie's glance.

'I'm going to draw up the drugs I need and

set up for a crash intubation,' he told her. 'I'll
need your help, so try and ignore whatever
else might happen, okay?'

Like the shouting that was happening outside only seconds later?

'Come out with your hands in the air,' she
heard a male voice command. 'We've got the
shed surrounded.'

'Oh, my…' Carla's mother had got to her
feet to stare out of the window. 'They've got
guns, those policemen.'

'Sit down, love.' Jonno's instruction sounded
like a casual invitation but Brie could hear a
thread of steel beneath it. 'You don't want to
distract anybody from doing their job out there
and it's probably best to stay out of sight. Have
you had your spray now?'

'Yes.'

'How's that chest pain?'

'Better.' She sank back onto the couch.
'Why isn't Carla waking up? What are you
doing?'

'She's having a little trouble with her breathing so we're going to help her by putting a
tube into her throat.' Jonno caught Brie's gaze
again. 'Ready?'

Brie nodded. She was. What was happening outside to secure the scene so that more
emergency personnel could come into the

house became a background hum. Even any concern for Carla's mother or for Simon was temporarily shelved. They had one job to do here that could very well save this woman's life and that one glance from Jonno had been enough for Brie to summon the confidence *she* needed.

She *could* do this.

Technically, she knew that a crash intubation was a way to rapidly sedate and paralyse a patient who needed airway protection because they couldn't maintain or protect their airway themselves.

'Right...' Jonno picked up a loaded syringe. 'Can you put some cricoid pressure on, please?'

Brie had done this many times, but only in training. Only on a mannequin. It felt very different to be doing it on a real person but she knew she was feeling for the hard, ring-like structure beneath the cricothyroid cartilage. She also knew that the manoeuvre was used to avoid aspiration of stomach contents that was the complication of airway management that carried the highest risk of fatality. She held the ring between her thumb and forefinger and applied pressure.

'That's the rocuroniumin,' Jonno murmured moments later. He picked up another one of the syringes he'd prepared. 'We wait fifteen seconds and then it's time to push the ketamine.'

We. They were a unit. A team. Brie liked that.

She knew to increase the pressure once the drugs had taken effect. Then Jonno tipped Carla's head back and, with the same smoothness and confidence with which he'd gained IV access, he inserted the laryngoscope into her mouth to get a view of her airway. Then he reached down, without taking his eyes off what he could see, and put his fingers over Brie's. She knew what he was doing even though nothing was said and she was aware of a fleeting memory of the jokes in training about doing BURP. Jonno needed backwards, upwards and to the right pressure on the cartilage, to help him see what he was doing more accurately. He was going to find the best position and then it would be her job to maintain it until the endotracheal tube was placed and the cuff inflated to keep it secure.

It seemed to be only seconds after Jonno had put her fingers in the right place that he pulled out the bougie wire from inside the tube, emptied the syringe full of air to inflate the cuff and then attached the bag mask to the end of the tube. He held the mask out for

Brie to take and then picked up the earpieces for the stethoscope hanging around his neck.

'Give her a few breaths while I check we're in the right place and then we'll get it all secured. Sounds like we're about to get company.'

The background hum suddenly came back into focus. The banging on the front door and someone calling and Simon's voice telling them he could unlock the door for them and yes...he thought it was safe to come in. There was someone coming in through the back door at the same time, calling to reassure them that they were the police and not a returning offender.

There was another paramedic crew coming in as well but, while Jonno acknowledged them, it was Brie he was talking to as he looked at the screen of the defibrillator.

'Still tachycardic at one twenty-two and her BP's still lower than I'd like, but her oxygen saturation is going up and her end tidal CO_2 is sitting at forty-two, which is just where we like it.' He smiled at Brie. 'Good job.'

It was then he turned to the new crew and began to bring them up to speed. Another ambulance crew arrived and then more police officers and the house became so crowded it was overwhelming. Carla's mother was being attended to, having a twelve lead ECG taken to rule out an evolving heart attack. Simon was being carefully assessed as well, but Brie was relieved to see that he was looking better than he had earlier. She stayed where she was, supporting Carla's breathing, until the chaos settled a bit and the new crew took over.

'Looks like your partner's got a good concussion,' a paramedic told her as she got to her feet and stepped out of the way so they could lift Carla onto a stretcher. 'He's going to need a scan and observation for a while. Are you going to be okay on your own to get your truck back to your station?'

Brie nodded. 'Of course. What about Carla's mother?'

'She's stable. No sign of an infarct and her chest pain's resolved. We've got another crew coming to transport her for a more thorough checkup, though. Jonno, are you okay to follow us in? We'll be heading for the Central Infirmary.'

'Sure thing. Right behind you.' He was packing up his kit but glanced up at Brie. 'Where's your station?'

'Not too far. I'm with Westwood Ambulance EMS.'

'No way. That's where I'm based at the moment. How come I haven't seen you around?'

Brie blew out a breath. 'Maybe because this is my first shift?'

A huff of breath that sounded very close to laughter escaped Jonno. 'Well, you've certainly jumped in at the deep end, haven't you?' He zipped up his kit and got to his feet. 'But you used to work in Control, didn't you? Ages ago? Before I headed offshore?'

'Mmm…' How hard would he need to rake through his memories to find what was demanding attention again inside Brie's head right now? That totally unforgettable night that still haunted her dreams—in a very good way?

Apparently not that long.

'I remember you,' Jonno said softly.

A flash of something in his eyes was gone as fast as it had appeared, but it had still been long enough for Brie to register that that attraction that had led to the most memorable night of her entire life might very well still be there on his part. There was no doubt it was still there on her side of the equation. The tingle that had been sparked by him remembering her name was nothing compared to the spear of sensation she was experiencing now. And she knew it had to be her imagination but her knees really *did* feel weak for a heartbeat.

Jonno seemed to be trying to hide a smile as he refocused and turned to follow the crew taking Carla from the house. 'How 'bout I come and find you back on station so we can catch up properly?'

He was gone before Brie could respond, but what on earth would she have said, anyway?

Good idea—it's been far too long? Or perhaps, *No, I don't think that would be a good idea at all. I didn't think you were ever coming back and now I'm not at all sure I want you finding out that you're the father of my son...*

CHAPTER TWO

'MUMMA'S HOME...'

The joy in the excited cry, as Brie opened the back door of her house and stepped into her kitchen, brought a smile to her face despite the fatigue and worry weighing her down.

The fiercely tight hug of a six-year-old's arms around her neck as she crouched down to where Felix was sitting in his wheelchair beside the kitchen table was so good it brought a lump to her throat. Or maybe that had something to do with this new knot of anxiety that had lodged in her belly since she'd found out that Jonno Morgan was back in town?

'Mumma, I did it all by myself today. I rode Bonnie all by myself.'

'Really?' Brie exaggerated her most impressed expression. 'Felix Henderson rode a horse all by himself?'

Felix was beaming as he nodded vigorously but his grandmother's smile was reassuring. 'Don't worry, I was walking on one side and Kylie was on the other.'

'But I did it myself,' Felix insisted. 'I held the reins and made Bonnie walk.' He sighed happily. 'I love Bonnie.' Then he held his arms up for another hug. 'I love you too, Mumma.'

Brie kissed her son's soft curls and straightened the red plastic frames of his glasses before she stood up. 'Love you too.' She ruffled the ears of the curly-haired dog gazing adoringly up at Felix—or was it the plate on the tray across the armrests of his wheelchair that their beloved pet was more interested in? 'You haven't been feeding Dennis any of Nana's lasagne, have you?'

Felix shook his head but he was still grinning. And Dennis was licking his lips.

'I had to make your favourite dinner.' It was Brie's mother, Elsie's, turn for a hug. 'We needed something to celebrate your first day on the road. How was it?'

'Unforgettable.' Brie summoned a smile. 'I'll fill you in when our famous Paralympian equestrian in the making goes to bed.'

'What's a 'questrian?' Felix asked.

'Someone who rides horses,' Elsie responded.

'That's *me*.' Felix was beaming again. 'And I know what the Paralympics is. That's for people like me too.'

'It totally is,' Brie agreed. 'But future famous equestrians have to eat their broccoli to make sure they're getting all their vitamins.'

'But I don't like broccoli.' Felix made it sound like a perfectly legitimate excuse not to eat the green vegetable still on his plate. Dennis was lying down now. He didn't like broccoli either.

'You know what to do, darling.' Elsie picked up a floret of broccoli and held it out by the stem. 'You're the dinosaur and this is the tree. Scare the world and eat it in one giant bite.'

'I think I could eat the rest of your lasagne in one giant bite,' Brie said. 'I'm *so* hungry.'

'Sit yourself down.' Elsie smiled. 'There's plenty of broccoli left for us too.'

'I'll take my uniform off first. And I'll run a bath for Felix. Why don't you put your feet up and have a glass of wine? You've had a busy day today too, with the RDA after school.'

Riding for the Disabled was only one of many therapeutic activities built into Felix's life and it was his absolute favourite. Mind you, he'd look this happy if he'd been to a physiotherapy session or speech therapy or his dance class. He'd been a happy little boy from the moment he'd arrived in the world, loving life despite—or was it because of— the extra challenges that came with having spina bifida?

Felix didn't need his wheelchair most of the time but it was useful for covering longer distances or when he needed a rest, such as when he'd had a big day including pony riding. He'd taken off his foot and ankle braces already and his crutches were propped up in the hallway so, a short while later, Brie carried her little boy up the stairs and supervised his undressing and climbing into the bath, which he'd become determined to do on his own lately.

It was hair-washing night tonight and Felix screwed his eyes tightly shut and tipped his head back so his mum could use the plastic beaker to sluice the shampoo foam away.

'On my face too.'

He opened his mouth to catch some of the waterfall and then sprayed the water out.

'Did you see my whale spout, Mumma?'

'I did, sweetheart.' Brie was laughing with him as she tipped a last beakerful of water over his head. 'Okay, I think you're squeaky clean. Let's get you out and into your jim-jams.'

Felix was yawning by the time she turned him round to dry his back. As always, something snagged at her heart as she saw the scars from his multiple surgeries, including one that had happened well before he'd been born—the one that had probably helped the most and had made Felix one of the lucky few spina bifida children who didn't have to live with major bowel or bladder issues.

He was almost falling asleep before Brie had read more than a couple of pages of his favourite story about a spotted Appaloosa pony called Nobby who ran away to join a circus. She turned on the night light—the one that made stars shine on the ceiling—pulled up his duvet and leaned down to plant a very soft kiss on the dark curls that smelt so deliciously of baby shampoo.

'Time for a wish?'

Felix nodded and they whispered their modified version of the rhyme together. *'Star light, star bright, first stars I see tonight. I wish I may, I wish I might, have the wish I wish tonight...'*

Brie felt her heart squeeze with her love for

him as she watched his little face scrunch up in concentration.

'What did you wish for, Bubba?'

'That I get to ride Bonnie again next time...'

His words trailed off and his face softened into sleep but Brie took another moment, just to look down on this small person she loved so much that the squeeze on her heart tightened enough to hurt—in a good way.

Felix had been a blessing from the time he'd taken his first breath. He loved the world and the world, especially his mother and grandmother, loved him back wholeheartedly. If she could help it, Brie was not about to let anything, or any*one*, change that in any way.

It was then that the new challenge she was so unexpectedly facing suddenly got a whole lot bigger. A whole lot scarier. So Brie did what she'd always done when she had something big and scary to face.

She went to find her mum.

Elsie Henderson had dipped in and out of her nursing career over the years. She'd stopped working when Brie was born and had then changed from hospital shift work to more child-friendly hours in the local medical centre when Brie started school. She'd gone back to a position at Bristol's Central Infirmary when Brie was in her teens but had stopped again when Felix was born, to support Brie as a single mother to a special needs child.

It was only recently that she'd gone back to work again, this time in Bristol's St Nicholas Children's Hospital, in her favourite role as a paediatric nurse. She was only planning to work part-time and she and Brie were working out how to juggle their shifts so that they could both work in the careers they loved because, as Elsie said, if they wanted to be the best parent and grandparent they could be, they had to look after their own needs as well and do things that they were passionate about. The immediate future promised to deliver the best of both worlds and they would not only be able to give Felix all the supportive parenting he could possibly need and give their own lives an extra, fulfilling direction, but it would also make them financially secure enough to meet any other needs he would be facing as he grew up.

But Elsie hadn't bargained on her daughter having such a dramatic start to her new career.

'I'm horrified,' she confessed. 'Are you sure you wouldn't rather go back to working in the control room? With your new training and experience on the road you'd be able to handle anything over the phone.'

Brie shook her head as she ate another bite of her lasagne. 'It would be even more impossible to be happy being sat behind a desk and trying to coach people—who've never been trained—to do CPR or stop a major haemorrhage. Can you imagine if it had been that woman's elderly mother, with her own chest pain, and I was trying to tell her how to keep her daughter alive until help arrived?'

'Thank goodness it *did* arrive as soon as it did. You must have been so relieved to see that critical care paramedic coming in.'

'Yeah...' Brie put her fork down, her appetite suddenly fading.

It took only a split second of silence for Elsie to realise there was something she wasn't being told. 'What's wrong, Brie?' she asked quietly.

There was no point in beating around the bush.

'Jonno's back in town. He was the critical care paramedic I was working with today.'

This time, the silence was much longer and a lot deeper. In fact, Elsie didn't say a word until she'd got up and opened the fridge.

'I'm going to break my own rule and have another glass of wine. Can I pour you one?'

Brie closed her eyes. She had a difficult conversation coming up. 'Yes, please. Just a small one.'

Elsie sat down at the table again. 'So... Jonno Morgan, huh?'

'Mmm...'

'He's not related to someone who works at St Nick's, is he? Anthony Morgan? The best paediatric cardiac surgeon in the city, they say. I haven't met him yet but I've been caring for a few of his patients and know how highly people think of him. He must be around the right age to have a son who would be in his thirties.'

Brie shook her head. 'That night I met Jonno, he told me he was leaving because there was nothing to keep him in Bristol. I can remember that he specifically said he had no family here.'

Elsie took a sip of her wine. 'I guess Morgan's hardly an unusual name.' She let her breath out in a sigh. 'So...what are you going to do, darling? When are you going to tell him?'

'I don't know,' Brie said. 'I don't know if I *should* tell him.'

Elsie looked shocked. 'You can't *not* tell him. He has a child. Felix has a father.'

Brie tried to swallow that beat of fear along

with her wine. 'It's not as if I didn't try and tell him when I found out I was pregnant. I did everything I could. Someone gave me his phone number but it had already been disconnected. Emails bounced back as undeliverable. When I finally found him on social media and asked him more than once to contact me, he never bothered responding. The messages never even got marked as having been read. And nobody here knew where he was by then. Everybody knew he'd gone to the Mount Everest base camp in Nepal but, by the time my snail mail letter got there, he must have moved on and the letter came back with a stamp saying to return it to the sender. Do you know, I think I've still got that letter somewhere? It arrived back after Felix was born.'

Brie shook her head slowly. 'Anyway…it was about the time I posted that letter that we found out about what was wrong with Felix and contacting Jonno didn't seem that important any longer. I had to make choices about whether I wanted to have in utero surgery or wait until after he was born or whether I was going to continue with the pregnancy, even. It was hard enough just for the two of us to have to face that.'

'I know…' Elsie reached out to touch her

daughter's arm with a sympathetic rub. 'It was a horrible time.'

'I stopped even trying to contact Jonno then because the last thing we needed was for anyone else to try and make a choice like that for me. And part of me didn't want to hear what Jonno would have said because I think I'd already made up my mind that I had to do whatever I could to save my baby.'

'How could you be so sure that you knew what he would have said?'

'Because of who he is?' Brie shrugged. 'I'd always heard about the way he pushed himself physically to the nth degree. Both in his training and his hobbies. It seemed a no-brainer that he might have thought that a life where you were too disabled to do the kind of things he's so passionate about would be a life that wasn't really worth living. What if he'd persuaded me that was true and Felix had never been born?'

Elsie smiled. 'That would never have happened. You've been as fiercely protective as a mother lion ever since you learned that your baby was going to need special help.'

'And maybe I still need to protect him now, Mum. What if I told Jonno and he wanted to see him? Or worse, wanted to be involved in his life?'

'He does have that right,' Elsie said quietly. 'And Felix has the right to know that he does have a father. He's old enough now to know that it's something missing from his life. One of these days he's going to start asking questions that we can't ignore or brush off by telling him that not everybody has a daddy they live with.'

'Never did me any harm not having a father,' Brie muttered.

'That's completely different and you know it. Your dad died before you were even born. I never had a day of not wishing he was here to meet you and see what a wonderful baby and little girl you were. And the young woman you grew into being. I could be completely honest and tell you that he would have loved you to bits.'

'Yeah…well…what if Jonno didn't think Felix was wonderful? Or love him to bits? If he couldn't see past the crutches or glasses? If Felix was made to feel…' Brie had to search for a word that could encompass everything she never wanted her son to have to feel. '…to feel *less* than who he really is…'

'At some point in life, that's something he's going to have to deal with.'

'I know. And he does already to some extent with those kids at school that have given him a hard time. But how much worse would it be if his dad turned out to be a kind of superhero who goes around saving lives and, in his spare time, jumps out of planes with a parachute or leaps off mountains to go hanggliding or does a bit of deep-sea diving or an iron man challenge in Hawaii?' Brie caught her breath, to stop the small avalanche of all the things she'd heard about Jonno Morgan before she'd even met him. 'What if…' she added quietly, 'Felix discovered he has a dad like other kids he knows and then that dad decides that he's going to go off on another adventure and leave town for the next seven years? How damaging would *that* be?'

Elsie looked as disturbed as Brie was feeling. They both knew what the right thing to do was but the need to protect Felix—and themselves—was paramount.

'Will you be seeing Jonno again?'

'He's working out of the same station. He said that he'd come and find me so we could catch up properly.'

Elsie bit her lip. 'How do you feel about that?'

Brie smiled wryly. Oh, there was a question…

She couldn't deny that part of her had felt thrilled that he remembered her name. Maybe she'd dreamed about Jonno—and that night—often enough over the years that it had made it easy for her body to remind her what his touch was like and wrap it up with the kind of yearning she would have when she woke from those dreams. But right now?

'Terrified,' Brie said aloud. 'What if someone tells him I've got a six-year-old kid?'

'He won't know anything unless you tell him.'

Brie swallowed hard. 'I have to, don't I? At some point, I'm going to have to tell him.'

Elsie didn't say anything but she reached out and covered Brie's hand with her own, a silent signal that the support was there for when she was ready to do the right thing.

She wasn't ready yet. Far from it.

'I'll have to find the right time,' she said quietly. 'I need to know how long he's planning to be around. How he might feel about finding out he's a father. For all I know, he could be married with kids that he *does* know about. There could be more people than just us that this might affect.'

'I hadn't thought of that,' Elsie conceded. 'But the longer you leave it, the harder it might get to tell him. At some point in the future, he might want to find out more about his father. What if he finds out that Jonno was living here and had never been told about his existence?'

Brie took a deep breath. 'I *will* tell him,' she promised. 'Just not yet.'

CHAPTER THREE

IT WAS JONNO'S idea and he ran it past the duty manager, Dave, first thing the next morning.

'Brie…ah…' It was only then that Jonno re-alised he'd never known her last name, which felt a bit weird given he knew so much else about her, physically, at least. Even seven years ago, he'd felt as if he knew her before he ever met her because her voice was so fa-miliar. He'd heard it on the radio so many times as he got dispatched to jobs and often kept her talking to get as much information as he could. It had been the first thing he'd recognised when he'd found himself in her company in a totally unexpected situation yesterday.

Brie had been one of the best dispatchers in the control room but he'd never expected her to turn out to be the most beautiful woman he'd ever seen when she'd turned up at his farewell party. That soft cascade of curls framing an elfin face that made her eyes look so huge. Eyes that he could see were reflecting the attraction simmering in the air between them.

'Henderson?' Dave raised his eyebrows. 'The newbie who got caught up in the violent offender incident yesterday?'

'That's the one.'

Dave let his breath out in a huff that was almost a chuckle. 'Her first shift as a graduate and not a trainee observer. That'll go down in station history. What about her?'

'How's her partner? Simon?'

'Nasty concussion. He could be off work for weeks. Fingers crossed he doesn't end up with post-concussion syndrome, which could keep him grounded for months.'

'Where are you going to put Brie? It'll be her second day shift today, yes?'

'Yeah. She'll be here any minute. I haven't decided, to be honest. We haven't got space on a crew with the kind of mentor I'd like her to have, but I don't want to take her off the front line and put her on a patient transfer ambulance. I can use her for cover but no one's called in sick today.'

'What about putting her with me?'

'What? You're in a rapid response vehicle.'

'It's not unusual to be a mentor at the same time.'

'Yeah, but that's for people about to complete their critical care training, not a complete newbie. And you go to jobs that could break someone without enough experience.'

'She didn't break yesterday. She did a good job. Why not let her get some real experience—when you haven't got any gaps to fill or until you find a suitable crew partner for her on a general truck?' Jonno smiled at the senior officer. 'I promise I won't break her.'

So that was why Jonno was waiting for Brie when she arrived on station that morning.

Or one of the reasons, anyway. The other was that he hadn't stopped thinking about her after work yesterday. He'd gone back to the apartment he was living in while he renovated it to get it ready for sale and it seemed that stripping wallpaper created a mindset that was like a time warp.

Hardly surprising given that particular room he was redecorating, but the sense of being sucked back in time was deeper than that. Seven years ago, he couldn't wait to escape. From this city. From this apartment that was like a symbol of the sham marriage and lifestyle his mother had maintained, but mostly he had to get away from the man who was making another attempt to be part of his life as a father figure, which was the absolute last thing Jonno needed. Or wanted.

He'd found his way in life by then and he was doing it on his own terms. With no family and especially no dependants, it didn't matter if he killed himself doing something stupid like a base dive or having a go in a jet-pack wingsuit, if he was ever lucky enough to have the chance to do that. He could spend all the money he still had left from his inheritance from his mother on his expensive adventure sports if that was what he wanted to do, but he could also get the satisfaction of working in an often action-packed job where he got to save lives.

Like yesterday.

By the time he was winding down, steaming, scraping and tearing shreds of paper from his bedroom walls, he was thinking about another benefit of being a lone wolf in his mid-thirties. He wasn't—and never had been—hemmed in by a committed relationship. Not that he put it about with reckless abandon or anything. No… Jonno was very particular about the women he chose to take to his bed, and if it was something special there was no harm in letting it carry on for a while. Not long enough to turn into something serious, of course, but long enough to enjoy every minute.

Brie had been something special.

Not that his memories of the unexpected night they'd spent together, in this very apartment, was even in the back of his mind when he'd made the suggestion that she rode with him in the rapid response vehicle for the next shift or two. He'd been impressed with how she'd handled herself yesterday and he had the feeling that Brie Henderson might be special in more ways than he knew about. Plus, he was curious about the woman who'd chosen to leave the safety of handling emergency calls from the other end of a telephone line to being on the front line.

He was even more curious when he saw Brie's shocked expression when she found out who she was going to be working with today. There was nervousness there, as well. Of the job?

Or of him?

He gave Brie his best smile. 'Don't worry,' he told her. 'I'll look after you.'

Being this close to Jonathon Morgan was... well, it was disturbing, that was what it was. On several levels.

One was that Brie was being driven faster than she would have believed possible through the heavy traffic of a big city on a busy weekday. Jonno's driving wasn't just fast, it was very clever. He seemed to have the ability to sense a complication like a panicked driver swerving the wrong way having just noticed a vehicle with lights and sirens right behind him, someone deciding to plough on through a junction to get out of the way, a delivery truck driver who threw open his door without looking and even a dog that had apparently appeared from nowhere. It was kind of like riding a roller coaster, Brie decided. Scary but undeniably rather thrilling.

On top of that, it felt as if fate was throwing them together. How weird was it that her crew partner had been injured on her first shift, there weren't any other gaps that needed filling on other crews and Jonno was on the rapid response vehicle that the station manager had decided to put her on for some extra experience.

Or had Jonno had something to do with that decision? Brie suspected it was not a common way to provide a rookie paramedic with some additional training.

Most of all, though, it was disturbing because it wasn't just the experienced, confident driving that was exciting.

It was being this close to Jonno. Thinking that perhaps it had been his idea that she rode along with him because *he* wanted to be this close to her? To pick up where he'd left off seven years ago, perhaps? Not that that was going to happen but it was, admittedly, flattering to think it might be even a part of the motivation behind this unexpected change in her duties.

The way Brie was feeling was like an emotional coin that kept flipping. Excited but then scared. Delighted but then super wary. Wishing she could be somewhere else—as far away as possible—but then feeling privileged to be this close and to have an opportunity to learn from the best.

There was nothing to suggest that Jonno had chosen to have her work with him either, and no hint of anything other than professional communication, but there hadn't exactly been any time for that to happen yet. This call had come in within minutes of the news that she would be second crew on this rapid response vehicle and this particularly fast ride was going to put them first on scene to a three-year-old child who had potentially swallowed a dangerous amount of his grand-father's heart medication.

'Just one or two tablets of a calcium chan-nel blocker like this one can be lethal to a ten-kilogram toddler,' Jonno said, giving a bus driver a wave as he overtook the vehicle that had been pulled out of their way. 'Cardiovas-cular medications are among the top twenty-five drugs for potentially toxic ingestion, but they're the third most common substance re-sulting in the death of a child under five years old.' He gave Brie a sideways glance as they turned off the motorway and headed into a residential suburb. 'What sort of symptoms should we be concerned about?'

'Cardiac effects to the heart rate and/or rhythm?'

'Yep. What else?' Jonno killed the siren as they found the street they were looking for.

Brie tried to remember her training mod-ule on poisoning. 'Blood pressure changes,' she said. 'Hypotension?'

'Yep. That's the most common symptom. Worst case scenario is a cardiovascular col-lapse so we'd better be prepared for anything.' Jonno switched off the beacons on their ve-hicle, turning his head to peer at house num-bers.

To her relief, there was no sign of an imminent cardiovascular collapse as they entered the house. The toddler was sitting happily in front of the television, in fact, watching a children's programme.

His mother was a lot less happy. 'I'm so glad you're here,' she said. 'I'm worried sick about George...'

'So what's happened?'

'I was getting my dad's pills ready for today. He's got dementia and he lives with us. So I had all the pills out to put into the little boxes and I heard him calling out in the bathroom.' George's mother looked distressed. 'He'd got confused over how to flush the loo and he was getting upset because the taxi was coming to take him to the day care group he goes to. Anyway... I was in there for a minute and then the taxi arrived, so he needed help to get to the gate, but I could hear that George was happy singing along with his programme. And then I came in here and there were pills everywhere from the bottle of Dad's heart medicine. I don't know how many are missing.'

The quirk of Jonno's eyebrow let Brie know he wasn't too worried himself yet. He went to crouch down by the little boy.

'Hey, George. Is this a good show?'

George nodded. He pointed at the screen,

where people dressed in colourful animal costumes were singing a song.

'I hear that you're a good singer.' Jonno sounded impressed.

George nodded again. 'I can touch my tummy!' he sang, along with someone in a penguin costume. His singing was enthusiastic but not at all tuneful. 'Pat, pat, pat...'

Jonno was grinning. It was easy to tell what the next line of the song was going to be, thanks to the actions of the person dressed as a tiger. 'I can touch my head,' he sang. 'Pat, pat, pat...'

'Have you noticed anything unusual about his behaviour?' Brie asked.

'No. But I know he's eaten some of the pills. I had to wipe some white stuff off his chin and I found a half chewed-up pill on the floor. See?'

'Can I see the label on the bottle? And the pill organiser? I should be able to see how many might be missing.' Brie had to smile as she saw that both Jonno and George were now doing the actions to the song, along with singing the lyrics.

'I can touch my toes, pat, pat, pat...'

Her smile wobbled then. Because she had a sudden image in her head of Jonno on the floor, playing with a child like this, only it wasn't with a patient. It was with his own son...

How much would Felix love to have a daddy who would engage with him like the way Jonno was with George? How much was missing from his life because he only had his mum and his nana?

Brie shoved the thought aside, focusing on the job at hand. She was confident Jonno would be quite satisfied with the information he was getting from his somewhat unique method of interacting with a young patient. If Brie had been using the paediatric assessment triangle of appearance, work of breathing and circulation, she would be confident that George's vital signs were all within normal parameters. He clearly had no issues with his breathing if he could sing like that, his skin colour was good and he seemed to be behaving like any other happy child would. On the other hand, she was unsure of what they would do next.

'I'm pretty sure there are two pills missing, not counting the half chewed one,' she reported to Jonno.

'Are they slow release?'

Brie checked the bottle. 'Yes.'

Jonno stood up, leaving George to pat his ears by himself. 'Let's give his face and hands

another wash,' he suggested to the mother.
'Just in case there's something still on his
skin. I'm going to call for someone to come
and take you into hospital as well, so that
George can be monitored for a few hours.'

'Oh, no... Do you think he's really sick?'

'He seems absolutely fine,' Jonno assured
her. 'But, because the pills are slow release, if
he has swallowed any, it could take longer for
any symptoms to show up. I'm sure you'll be
happier to be somewhere that people can keep
a close eye on George. While we're waiting,
Brie and I will see if we can get an ECG, just
to make sure his heart's doing exactly what
it's supposed to.'

Brie opened the pouch on the side of the
defibrillator to find the packet of electrodes as
Jonno made a call requesting an ambulance
to transport mother and child to hospital.

'I've got a new game,' Jonno told George
as his mother was wiping his face and hands
with a damp cloth. 'Can you touch your chest?
Pat, pat, pat? Good boy... Do you want some
special stickers to go on your chest?'

George nodded eagerly.

'Okay... Mum's going to take your tee shirt
off and then Brie's going to help me put the
special stickers on. Oh...look at that...' A
small white pill rolled out of the elastic waist-

band of George's pants as the tee shirt was pulled out. Jonno picked it up and handed it to Brie. 'Only one missing now,' he said.

George could see what he was holding. 'Yucky,' he said.

'Sure is,' Jonno agreed. 'Did you try and eat them, George?'

George avoided his gaze and shook his head firmly. 'Too yucky.'

Jonno's lips twitched. 'Time for the sticker game,' he said. 'Can you lie as flat as a pancake on the floor? Show me where the stickers are going to go? And Mum? Maybe you could pack a bag with some toys and snacks and things that you might need with a few hours in the observation ward?'

By the time they had the ECG recorded, an ambulance had arrived to transport George and his mum to hospital.

'He could still develop symptoms, couldn't he?' Brie asked as they headed back to station, having transferred the care of their patient and seen them both into the ambulance. 'Especially for slow-release medications?'

'They'll keep a close eye on him for about six hours. If nothing's happened by then, he should be fine. If something shows up soon, they may give him some activated charcoal but that should be within the first hour or so of ingestion.'

Brie could see the ambulance turning onto the motorway ahead of them. 'You're really good with kids,' she said. 'I can imagine getting an ECG on most toddlers could be a bit tricky.'

'Maybe I've never grown up properly myself.' Jonno threw her a grin. 'And I love kids.'

Oh... Brie's heart skipped a beat. She couldn't help the flash of fantasy that was an extension of imagining Jonno playing with Felix. This time, it was an image of them all together. As a family...

Maybe she should have tried harder to contact him.

Maybe it wasn't too late?

Her mother was right. The longer she left it, the harder it was going to become.

She took a deep breath and hoped she would be able to sound as if her question was simply a response to what he'd just told her.

'So...you've got some of your own now?'

'What...*kids*?' Jonno sounded horrified. 'Not that I know of. Thank goodness.'

The fantasy crashed and burned.

'I love them when they're someone else's,' he added. 'That way, they don't mess with the stuff I love to do.'

Brie managed to find a smile. 'You mean travelling? Having adventures?'

'Absolutely. And doing the kind of things that you'd never do if you had anyone dependent on you like a wife or kids. You know… like flying with one of those jet-pack wingsuits? Have you seen the video that came out recently of that guy flying beside a passenger jet in Dubai?' The gleam in Jonno's eyes advertised both admiration and envy. 'Crazy…'

Brie shook her head. 'No, I haven't seen it.'

'I'll show you later. I've got it downloaded on my phone.' Jonno's attention seemed to be caught by a hardware shop they were passing. 'That reminds me. I've got to get some paint after work today. I've nearly finished stripping the wallpaper in my bedroom. Maybe I should get your advice about a good colour?'

Brie looked out of her window to avoid meeting any glance that might be coming her way. At some point, it was inevitable that something was going to be said about the time that Brie had been in that room. About the unprecedented—on her part, anyway—passionate encounter they'd shared.

The fact that they had a past history, albeit very fleeting, was there, simmering away between them beneath the professional veneer, as if they might both be waiting for a signal that it didn't need to be a secret.

'I didn't have you pegged as a DIY type,' she said lightly.

'I'm not. I'd rather be racing planes like a superhero, to tell the truth. But I need to sell the apartment. It's my last tie to Bristol and when it's gone, I'll be gone too. For good, this time.'

Brie took a moment longer before she let him see her face. Any inclination to tell Jonno about his son right now was evaporating as convincingly as that snapshot of a happy family including a daddy for Felix. Telling him at all was becoming even more of an issue, in fact. Jonno had no intention of hanging around for very long at all so it would only break a little boy's heart if he found out he had an amazing father, who actually *was* a superhero in real life, only to have him vanish again.

'I'm only filling in as a locum here,' Jonno added. 'It's a race to see whether I'll get the apartment sold or be out of a job first. Not that it matters when the prize is the same— a fresh start. A new adventure. I'm thinking maybe Australia. Or New Zealand. Did you know that Queenstown, in New Zealand, is the adventure capital of the world?'

'No, I didn't know that.'

'I haven't tried bungee jumping yet.'

'I'm happy to say that I never want to.' It was easier for Brie to find a smile this time because it felt as if the decision of whether or not to tell Jonno he was a father was being made for her and it was proving to be a huge relief. Maybe she had the perfect excuse not to tell him, seeing as he was going to be on the other side of the globe very soon and would never be coming back. If Felix ever tracked him down in decades to come she could honestly say that keeping silent had been to protect him. To protect everybody involved, in fact, because the last thing Jonno wanted was to have a continued connection to Bristol.

It's my last tie to Bristol and when it's gone, I'll be gone too. For good, this time...

'So...' After the outbound journey from station on the way to the potential paediatric poisoning, it felt as if Jonno was driving super slowly now. His smile was just as relaxed. 'What do you reckon? About the colour I should paint my bedroom? I'm thinking a nice strong colour like aubergine or a dark blue. Mind you, even a lurid pink or something would be better than the wallpaper that was there. Don't suppose you remember those things that looked like up-side-down pineapples?'

And there it was...

The window into one single night that had happened a very long time ago, but Brie could remember every single detail. Including the hideous wallpaper in Jonno's bedroom and the first words he ever said to her that weren't over the radio.

'You're Brie, right? Like the cheese?'

'Yeah...like the cheese.'

'I feel like I know you... But I've never seen you before. How crazy is this?'

'Same. I've heard your voice on almost every shift I've done.'

'You've always looked after me. Dispatching me to the best jobs and trying to make sure we got enough of a break to get something to eat.'

The noise of the rowdy private party happening in a local pub was all around them but, for Brie, it was nothing more than static. A fuzziness in the background of the real picture. She was meeting Jonno Morgan, a medic who was universally admired and respected throughout Bristol's emergency services and...he fancied her.

'I wish I'd known...'

'Known what?'

'How gorgeous you are...' He touched her face with a single fingertip, tracing a line from her eyebrow to skirt her cheekbone and then slide to her mouth, where it paused for a heartbeat at the corner before skimming her bottom lip.

'Same...'

Brie knew she was blushing but she'd always been so shy when it came to talking to men. She would never have dreamed of flirting like this with anyone, let alone Jonno. Perhaps being dragged to this party by a friend from the control room without being given time to find an excuse had something to do with a new confidence. More likely, it was due to the second glass of wine she'd just finished—or had that been the third? The fact that Jonno was so attracted to her was probably due to the amount he'd had to drink as well, but Brie didn't care. Because she'd never felt like this before. As if she was actually desirable—to someone like Jonno Morgan?

'Let me get you another one of those.'

Jonno's hand was over Brie's, about to take possession of the empty glass, but then it stopped and she knew why.

She could feel it too. The jolt like an elec-

tric shock as their hands touched. The heat that was being generated by the prolonged contact.

Brie couldn't look away.

'I want to kiss you,' Jonno said, and he was probably shouting, given the noise of the party around them, but it felt as if he were whispering in her ear. 'But not here...'

He took the glass from her hand and put it down on the nearest table, and then his hand was holding hers again.

'I live just round the corner,' he said. 'How 'bout we find somewhere quieter so we can get to know each other a bit better?'

'But this is your party.'

'Nobody will miss me. They're all having far too good a time. And, hey...if it's my party, don't I get to choose to be with the person I most want to be with?'

There was no one Brie wanted to be with more than Jonno. Who wouldn't want to find themselves in a real-life fantasy with someone they'd had a crush on from the moment they'd heard their voice over the radio? They were both adults. Both single. She didn't even have to worry about something as mundane as birth control because she'd been on the pill for months now, to try and regulate an annoyingly unpredictable cycle.

Jonno bought a bottle of champagne on the way out. They held hands as they walked to his apartment. They drank the champagne and talked as if they'd known each other for years. They laughed about the upside-down pineapples on the wallpaper in his bedroom.

And then they didn't talk again.

Dawn was breaking outside when Jonno finally fell asleep. Brie was still awake, still stunned by the wildest and yet the most attentive lovemaking she'd ever experienced. Every cell in her body was still humming and her head was spinning, but maybe that was the last of that champagne catching up with her and pushing her over the edge.

When her stomach started tying itself in knots, she slipped quietly from Jonno's bed and carried her clothes in her arms to get dressed downstairs. To escape before she could spoil the most perfect night in her life, and a fantasy that had exceeded all expectations, by throwing up everywhere...

Perhaps it was because Brie had relived that fantasy so many times over the years since that night that it could flash through her mind in a tumble of images and emotions that took no longer than the blink of an eye.

'Definitely not aubergine...' Brie made it

sound as if she'd given the query about paint colour some careful thought and she caught Jonno's gaze briefly so that she could make her denial more convincing. 'And no... I don't remember the pineapples but they do sound truly awful.'

He knew she was lying.

It was unfortunate that they were queued behind the traffic at a red light because it meant that Jonno didn't have to look away in a hurry. Brie could feel her cheeks getting pink. She'd never been any good at lying.

Jonno knew she remembered.

And the way his eyes seemed to become an even darker shade of brown sent a spear of sensation right through her body. She'd seen Jonno's eyes darken like that before. Before he'd kissed her for the first time...

He wanted to kiss her again.

And, heaven help her, but Brie wanted him to.

Perhaps heaven did help her because the radio crackled into life at that exact moment.

'Echo One...how do you read?'

Jonno was still holding Brie's gaze as he responded. 'Loud and clear, Control.'

'We're dropping a job on you. Cardiac arrest. Dog walker at the south end of Castle

Park. Bystander CPR underway. Details coming through...'

'Roger that...'

Jonno switched on the beacons and eased the vehicle out of the stalled traffic. By the time he did a U-turn and activated the siren, that conversation with Brie was clearly forgotten.

And thank goodness for that.

It was still there.

That extraordinary attraction that had pulled them together for a night that Jonno had never forgotten.

He'd never forgotten that stab of disappointment when he'd woken up to find he was alone in his bed. Why hadn't she stayed? Not being able to say goodbye, let alone tell her that it had been the best night of his life, had left him with the feeling that he was leaving town with something unfinished.

Something important.

But there was nothing he could have done about it. He had to get his bag packed, hand over the keys to his apartment to the agency who would be managing the rental and get to the airport. He would be winging his way to Nepal in a matter of hours, with a group of climbers who had employed him to stay at base camp as their medic while they made possibly more than a single attempt to climb Mount Everest.

One adventure had led to another as Jonno became known for being the best in the business and prepared to take on even the wildest terrain. He'd meant to come back ages ago to sort out the loose end in his life that his apartment represented. The last thing he'd expected was to find that he still had that other loose end—the woman who'd rocked his world and then vanished into the night like a puff of smoke from a fantasy that had just imploded.

Maybe he would have simply let it go when Brie told him she didn't remember—or didn't want to remember—her visit to his apartment, but then he'd seen the colour creep into her cheeks.

The way it had at that party, when he'd finally shaken off so many well-wishers and managed to capture the attention of the most beautiful woman he'd ever seen. He'd known then that she was lying about not remembering. Perhaps there was unfinished business there for her too?

Jonno was here to make sure he could leave this city for good with no regrets. If there was a chance that he could revisit that fantasy and give it the kind of ending it should have had the first time, perhaps for both of them, well…why not? Life was short and his time in Bristol was even shorter.

But something was telling Jonno that there could be a good reason for Brie to not want to go jogging down memory lane with him, and he knew that was most likely because she was no longer single. Or had she fled that night because she hadn't been single then? No… Jonno threw that idea out. He was a good judge of character and he would never have picked the Brie he'd met that night as someone who would cheat on a partner.

That didn't mean she was still single now, of course. She wasn't wearing a wedding ring but that didn't mean much, did it? You could be in a committed relationship with someone without ever getting married. Jonno fully intended finding out but he didn't get a chance to try and satisfy his curiosity until a rather busy shift was ending.

'Come and look at this, Brie.' He tapped the triangle on his screen. 'It's the wingsuit video I was telling you about.'

'Wow…' Brie's eyes widened as she saw the improbable clip of a human flying alongside an enormous passenger jet.

'That's an Airbus A380,' Jonno told her. 'Biggest plane in the world.'

'Unbelievable…' Brie shook her head. 'And you're planning to do that?'

He grinned. 'It's on my bucket list, that's for sure. There's a few logistics to work out, like how much it would cost.' He put his phone away. 'You heading straight home?' If she wasn't, Jonno intended to suggest they went somewhere for a drink. Or coffee. Or anything that would give them some time together away from work.

But Brie nodded. 'Yeah… I need to run. That last job has made me a bit later than usual.'

'Dependants, huh?' Jonno tried to make it sound like a good thing. 'I never did ask whether *you* had kids by now. Or a husband.'

'No husband.' Brie was heading towards the locker room. 'But I do live with someone.' She threw a smile over her shoulder. 'And Dennis the menace, of course.'

'How old is Dennis?'

'Almost four.'

Wow…

The stab of disappointment was real.

Oddly, it was even sharper than the one he remembered from waking up to find she'd vanished from his bed.

But that was that. Jonno had a firm rule not to get involved with anyone who was in a relationship.

Even if he knew damn well that she was still attracted to him...

CHAPTER FOUR

IT HADN'T REALLY been a lie.

She'd just fudged the truth a little.

So why did she feel as if she'd made a huge mistake? Done something unforgivable, even?

Brie *did* live with an almost four-year-old called Dennis. And she was living with someone in a relationship that had not only given her the support to be the kind of single mother to a special needs child that she could be proud of, but had even accommodated her training in the career she'd dreamed of for years. The new adjustment to her shift work was working well so far too.

Brie got to have a day with Felix the next day, after her mother had left early to work a day shift on the paediatric surgical ward. Having done two day shifts herself, Brie had the first of two nights to work, which meant she had her day clear to take Felix to school in the morning and to a physiotherapy session in the afternoon. There were no out-of-school activities scheduled for tomorrow, which was a good thing, as Elsie was working another day shift and Brie would have to sleep during school hours to be ready for her second night shift.

Any day, like today, that included a session in the specialised physiotherapy hot pool was always a treat. With the heat of a comfortable bath and the reduction of gravity the water provided, the range of movement and stamina exercises were so much easier and more fun that it had been a favourite since Felix had been a toddler. Brie loved seeing the grin that never faded and hearing the way his shrieks of laughter echoed in the tiled pool area.

The pleasure was more than a little dampened today, however, by the guilt that Brie was struggling with. The conversation she'd had with her mother last night had an echo far less agreeable than Felix's laughter.

'You still have to tell him,' Elsie had said. *'Even if he's not planning to be around for long. You never know—he might change his mind when he knows. You have to do the right thing.'*

'But it has to be at the right time. We might have been working together today, but it's

*hardly the appropriate time to drop a bomb-
shell like that on someone.'*

*'So, find a way to spend some time with
him away from work. Go out to dinner or
something. I'll babysit.'*

*'Mum! I'm not going to ask Jonno out to
dinner!'*

At least Brie didn't have to let her mind
wander in the direction of the 'or something'
her mother had suggested. The way the atmosphere had changed the moment she'd told
Jonno that she was living with someone—
and, okay, had deliberately given the impression that she had a child called Dennis—had
been palpable. Any hint that he might be
thinking they could pick up where they'd left
off seven years ago had disappeared like the
flame of a snuffed-out candle.

She'd known she was completely safe at
that point. She would have been disappointed,
in fact, if Jonno Morgan hadn't made it obvious that someone being in a relationship was
a no-go area for him. She'd always thought
of him as one of the 'good' guys. The kind
you'd dream of having as a partner.

Or a father for your child?

Yes, but not if it presented a danger to a
world that she had poured her heart and soul
into creating for her son. And Jonno did pres-

ent a danger. He could break her son's heart by walking out on him—or getting killed. For heaven's sake, she just had to remember the video he'd shown her of the person flying beside that huge plane to have her blood run cold at the thought of Felix watching his father doing something that dangerous.

And, while it was less important, there was a personal danger there as well, because Brie knew that the attraction that had led to Felix being part of her life in the first place was still very much alive and kicking. Not just undiminished but quite possibly enhanced beyond reality because her memories of that night were the closest thing Brie had had to a sex life since she'd become a mother. That pull—which could magnify the new complication in her life—could not be allowed to develop any further.

But did that justify the barrier she had deliberately put up to protect both herself and Felix?

The fudging of the truth that, okay, most people would consider a lie, wasn't sitting at all well with Brie.

Having Jonno smile at her as she arrived on station that evening made it quite clear to Brie that she had made a mistake. Instinct told her that Jonno had never been anything other than honest with her and he didn't deserve to be treated with any less respect himself.

But how could she put things right?

She certainly wasn't going to get an opportunity on this shift because someone had called in sick and she was put on an ambulance with another paramedic, Liz, an experienced medic in her late forties. It was a busy night but none of their callouts involved trauma or medical events serious enough to request advanced backup so Brie didn't even see Jonno again until nearly seven a.m. when her shift was finishing and the station locker room was busy with people both arriving and preparing to leave.

'I need coffee,' Liz declared, closing her locker. 'A real coffee. Anyone fancy coming out to breakfast?'

'Sure. Count me in.' Jonno looked as though he'd managed to catch some sleep overnight. He looked, in fact, as if he'd just got out of bed, with his hair all rumpled and some designer stubble shading his jaw. And he was smiling at Liz but Brie could feel something deep inside her own body trying its best to melt.

He looked…impossibly gorgeous…

'Brie?'

'Sorry, Liz, I've got to get home.' Brie pulled her bag from her locker and checked that her car keys were inside.

'To Dennis,' Jonno supplied helpfully.

'Mmm…' Brie bit her lip. 'He'll be wanting his breakfast.'

Jonno blinked at her but Liz actually laughed. 'You called your kid *Dennis*?'

'Not exactly,' Brie admitted. 'Dennis is a fur baby. Bit of everything, including some poodle. Very cute, but he was a very naughty puppy. Dennis the menace seemed to suit him.'

'Dennis is a *dog*?' Jonno stepped out of the way of someone reaching past him to open a locker and that put him right beside Brie as she turned to walk out. 'And the person you're living with? Is he just a flatmate?'

'Um…not exactly.' Brie didn't dare catch Jonno's gaze. 'I ended up moving back home a few years ago so I'm living with my mum again.'

Tell him, said the small voice at the back of her head. *Here's your chance…*

Except it wasn't a chance. She couldn't just tell him she had a six-year-old child without the possibility that he'd do the maths instantly and be blindsided in front of the people he was currently working with. That was hardly treating him with the respect he deserved, was it?

The scramble of Brie's thoughts was making her walk faster towards the main doors of the station but Jonno's long legs were keeping up with her effortlessly. Then he dropped back slightly as he slowed his steps.

'Wait a minute…' he called softly.

Brie found herself instantly slowing her own pace.

'Are you telling me you don't have a partner?' Jonno's voice was quiet behind her but she could hear him clearly. 'That you're…single? Why on earth did you want me to think that you weren't?'

'Um…' Brie stopped in her tracks, mortified. She had never blushed quite this hard, judging by the level of heat she could feel in her face, and she didn't dare look back. Until she heard the huff of sound from Jonno that was almost laughter.

'I get it,' he murmured. 'And I know…it's weird, right? I wasn't expecting it either…'

Brie tried to pull in a breath as she met his gaze but it felt as if most of the oxygen in this building had been used up. That might also explain why her response came out sounding slightly hoarse.

'What is?'

'That it's still there,' Jonno said.

Brie wasn't going to ask what he meant. She didn't need to because she knew exactly what was still there. That once-in-a-lifetime, totally irresistible attraction that was equal enough on both sides to pull them together with all the force of a human nuclear reaction if they got close enough.

She could see the gleam in Jonno's eyes that suggested he would be up for getting that close—if she was. A gleam that told her she wasn't anywhere near as safe as she'd thought she was this morning. A gleam that scrambled her brain enough to want things that she couldn't—or *shouldn't*—have. Especially not with this particular man.

Liz overtook them. 'You coming, Jonno? I can smell the coffee from here. Some bacon and eggs too...'

Jonno's smile was lazy. 'Lead the way.' He walked past Brie. He didn't have to say anything more. That subtle almost wink he gave her as he passed was enough to let her know that their conversation was nowhere near finished.

It was that lazy smile that stayed with Brie as she tried to top up on her sleep once Felix was safely delivered to school.

Or maybe it was the confidence that was behind it. Did Jonno think that it was inevitable that she would end up in his bed again? That this was just some kind of game and that, if he played it without breaking too many rules, he was bound to win. Because things had probably always worked out like that for him?

Well…not this time.

Even when just the thought of being with Jonno—being kissed, or…dear Lord, being touched by him—was creating havoc in various parts of her body and making it impossible to get her mind anywhere near the quiet space it needed in order to slide into sleep. Part of that havoc was a small voice that seemed to be gaining enough of an audience to make it refuse to go away.

How long? it was asking. *How long is it since you felt like this?*

The answer was built into the reason the question was being asked. Brie knew perfectly well that there had only ever been one man who'd made her feel like this. As if every cell in her body had woken up and was quietly fizzing. Waiting for that kiss. That touch.

No. It couldn't happen. Brie wasn't a single young woman now, with the freedom to do whatever she wanted and to follow her heart's desire. She was a mother. And a paramedic. Her life was all about being responsible and supporting other people, especially those she cared most about. Even allowing herself to sink into these feelings at all felt somehow wrong. Selfish. So she couldn't afford to play games with Jonno, even if she was reasonably confident she could stop him winning in the end.

Even when she found she was crewed with Jonno again on her next shift, which meant they were going to be spending an entire night together. Because this was work. The professional arena where any kind of personal games were not only inappropriate, it would be unforgivable if they interfered with patient care in any way.

What Brie hadn't bargained on was that Jonno seemed to be prepared to play a long game. When they found themselves alone in the staffroom, waiting for their first call, there was no hint of flirting in the glance that grazed Brie's. He looked…curious.

'So… Dave tells me you left your job in Control not long after I went off to the Himalayas. How come?'

'I needed a break.' Brie's heart rate kicked

up, both at the idea that Jonno had been asking about her and because this could be exactly the opportunity she needed. Was this the way it would happen? That the truth would emerge in a casual conversation? She cleared her throat. 'I had a few…um…health issues.'

She could actually feel Jonno's focus narrowing. That brilliant mind of his was probably throwing up all sorts of possible 'issues', including those involving mental health. He would be offering her the respect of not asking questions she might not want to answer but there was no doubt that he was interested. Concerned, even.

Because he *cared* about her? As more than simply a long-ago one-night stand?

Oh, help…the feeling of being cared about was almost as seductive as being desired.

But she couldn't tell him about Felix right now. They were on the start of a shift and messing with his head with something that huge would be a distraction for the rest of the night. She had no idea how to start telling him, anyway. The words were dancing in her head like fireflies that would be too hard to catch.

Jonno's calm voice was easy to focus on. 'But you're okay now?'

'Never better,' Brie assured him.

'Good to hear.' That focus in his eyes softened with a warmth Brie could feel right down to her toes.

'And you decided to train as a paramedic instead of going back to the control room? That was a big change to make.'

Brie nodded. This was safe ground. 'It had never occurred to me that I could be brave enough to be out there on the road, dealing with the kind of scenarios I was hearing about in those frantic triple nine calls for help but, you know, it got more and more frustrating when the calls got disconnected as soon as an ambulance, or someone like you, arrived. Or worse, when speaker phone was left on and I was listening to what was going on and then another call would come in so I was the one who had to disconnect and start all over again, trying to calm a panicked person enough to get the information needed to dispatch another crew.'

At some point, as Brie was talking to Jonno and he was nodding his understanding of why her old job had become so frustrating, something clicked in the back of Brie's mind. There were two separate things going on here, which was making everything so much more complicated.

There was her attraction to Jonno that she knew was still there, on both sides.

And there was the fact that Jonno had a son he didn't know he had.

Telling him something that was going to change his life—possibly in a way that would make him unhappy or angry, even—was a far more difficult prospect than dealing with any sexual tension that was, in fact, rather surprisingly delicious...

It wasn't that she was never going to tell him. It was, as she'd explained to her mother, a matter of choosing the right time. Maybe she *did* need to find a way to spend some time with Jonno away from work. Perhaps, if this *was* some kind of personal game, the card with Felix on it needed to be slipped up her sleeve for now, leaving Brie to play with the cards she was already holding, which were purely about each other.

One of them was also about this new space in her life. An adult, child-free space that was completely separate to her life as a mother and a daughter. This was an independent space that was about who she was in her own right—the core of the person she'd always been, before she'd willingly given up so much for her baby. And, somewhere in that core, was a yearning that Brie hadn't actually acknowledged. A need for something that was missing from her life? Something that it had taken Jonno's sudden appearance to bring to the surface?

Something her mother had said in the wake of Jonno's return popped into the back of Brie's mind. About how, if she wanted to be the best parent she could be, she had to look after her own needs as well. Could one of those needs be as simple as a physical connection with someone? A sex life?

Maybe she was being offered an opportunity to find out the answer to that question and, if it was something really important she was missing, maybe it was time to think about dating again. Starting a search for a life partner—something she knew Jonno Morgan could never have been because any dependants were the last thing he wanted in his own life.

That didn't necessarily mean Jonno couldn't help her discover the answer to this new question of how much a gap not having a relationship was creating in her life. Hypothetically, of course. Having the father of her child around was quite complicated enough without allowing this attraction to get out of control.

* * *

Something wasn't quite adding up and it was making Jonno cautious.

Why was Brie so wary of being close to him?

It was almost as if she had been—was *still*, even—upset about what had happened all those years ago, but that didn't make sense. She'd known it was his last night in town so it was never going to be the start of anything. It had been a memorable night, but that was all it could have ever been. Surely Brie hadn't expected him to stay in touch afterwards? He'd given up on using social media because the patch of the globe he was heading towards didn't allow for easy communication with anybody. He'd had enough trouble getting a phone and email connection to work. He'd discovered he didn't miss social media at all and, while he'd still thought of Brie surprisingly often, he had no real desire to contact her again. Because he didn't do relationships. Besides, Brie had been the one to disappear without saying goodbye—or even leaving him her phone number.

But now he was curious, dammit. Even more so now that he knew she was single. What kind of health issues had she had? And why on earth was she living with her mother?

Jonno couldn't imagine being in the same room with his father, let alone sharing the house he'd grown up in, a huge old dwelling with an even bigger garden in one of the leafy, more affluent suburbs in Bristol, where you might expect a renowned paediatric cardiac surgeon to reside.

He didn't want to push too hard, however. He already knew how disappointing it was to have Brie vanish without a trace and while that couldn't physically happen while they were working together, it could happen on a personal connection level and Jonno wanted to avoid that. Because he was curious. And because he was still attracted to her in a way he hadn't been to any woman, before or since that one night with Brie Henderson. Had it really been as amazing as he remembered it being or had he dreamt even a part of what had exploded between them?

One thing he could be sure of was that Brie was passionate about her new career and that was obviously going to be an easy way to reconnect with her safely. Being in a position to give her the chance to consolidate and expand her skills exponentially by being involved in critical cases was a gift he was only too happy to offer. And Brie was clearly equally happy to accept.

He saw the way her eyes lit up with the priority call they got just after midnight that night.

'Sixty-eight-year-old female with severe, ten out of ten, left-sided abdominal pain. Conscious and breathing.' Jonno glanced at the GPS route highlighted on the dashboard screen as the automatic gates slid open from the station entrance. 'First thoughts?'

'Too many,' Brie confessed. 'Renal colic? Bowel obstruction? Ruptured appendix? Any other information?'

'Her GP increased her blood pressure medication a couple of days ago after she went to him with a bad headache.'

'Ah…' Brie was chewing her lip. 'Do we know if the onset of the pain was sudden?'

'Good question.' Jonno nodded approvingly and then responded to the person in the control room, telling him an ambulance was being sent as backup for transport but could be ten minutes behind them. 'Roger that,' he said. 'Our ETA is currently six minutes.'

Brie was waiting for him to finish the exchange. 'Triple A?' she suggested. 'Acute coronary syndrome? Thoracic aortic dissection?'

Jonno nodded again. 'My guess is a triple A.'

'An abdominal aortic aneurysm,' Brie said

slowly. 'If it's ruptured, we might well be too late.'

'Let's hope it's just a dissection. What's the difference?'

'An aneurysm is a bulge in an artery wall where it's weaker. A dissection is where the wall tears and blood leaks between the layers of the artery wall. A rupture is when all the layers tear and it can lead to massive internal bleeding that's very likely to be fatal.'

'What would be a major diagnostic factor to look for?'

'A pulsatile mass in the abdomen?'

'Which may or may not be obvious. Depending on how distressed our patient is, I'll get you involved in the assessment.'

'Okay.'

He could actually hear the way Brie sucked in her breath, preparing herself for anything, and it almost made him smile. He'd been that new once. Scared of what he might find when he arrived on scene but so determined to do whatever he could to save a life.

An extremely anxious husband was waiting for them at the address and took them straight to their patient, Maria. She was lying on her bed, constantly shifting with the pain, sweating, very pale and clearly terrified.

'I'm Jonno,' he introduced himself. 'And

I've got Brie with me. We're going to have a quick look at you and do something for that pain you're in and then we're going to get you to hospital as quickly as we can.' He hoped his smile was reassuring. 'Can I have a look at your tummy while Brie puts some sticky patches on so we can see what your heart's up to?'

Maria nodded. So did her husband. 'Please,' he begged. 'Do whatever you can. I've never seen her like this before.'

Brie was opening the pouches on the defibrillator cover, preparing to get a set of vital signs and a rhythm strip. Maria was in too much distress for it to be appropriate to let Brie take part in an urgent assessment and treatment but he knew she would be soaking it all in and they could spend all the time they needed later to go over every detail.

Jonno uncovered Maria's abdomen and gently laid his hand on the first quadrant he was going to palpate on the other side to where the pain was located.

'Tell me about this pain,' he said. 'Can you describe it?'

'Like something was tearing.'

'Are you having any chest pain as well?'

'No… I don't think so.'

It wasn't easy to assess her abdomen because Maria was unable to stay still due to the pain, but Jonno had moved his hand to her left side and he could feel the unmistakable pulsing beneath his palm.

'Have you ever been assessed for an abdominal aneurysm?' he asked.

It was her husband that answered as Maria groaned and rolled her head to one side.

'Yes,' he said. 'But they said it was only small and shouldn't be a problem, especially if she stopped smoking. They said they'd keep an eye on it.'

Smoking, along with high blood pressure were two of the biggest risk factors for a complication like this.

'Is that what's causing this?' Maria's husband sounded alarmed.

'I think so.' Jonno caught his gaze and could see that the man was well aware of how serious this situation was. He reached for his wife's hand.

'Heart rate's sixty-four,' Brie told him. 'Sinus rhythm with a few ectopic beats. Blood pressure's one ninety over one hundred and four, and the oxygen saturation's down to ninety-two percent.'

'Let's get an oxygen mask on,' Jonno said. 'And I'll get you to help hold her arm still for me so that we can get an IV line in.' He

leaned down. 'Maria? I'm going to put a needle in your arm so that we can give you something for the pain, okay?'

Maria's response was another agonised
groan but she nodded. Her husband had tears
on his face but his voice was calm.

'I'm here, my love,' he told his wife. 'I'm
right here...'

Brie drove the rapid response vehicle so that
Jonno could travel in the ambulance with
their patient with the triple A dissection.
Maria was still alive when they got her to
hospital and they bypassed the emergency
department to get straight to Theatre, where
a surgical team was waiting for her.

Jonno went over the dramatic case with
her in the kind of detail that reminded Brie of
swotting for her exams, but it felt even more
satisfying to know that she was achieving a
great score. And it wasn't the only benefit
of being crewed with someone who was so
knowledgeable.

There was more drama to come that night,
with a night worker at a processing plant am-
putating several fingers and an employee
getting knocked off his bicycle as he went
to start work at a bakery just before dawn.
Brie followed the ambulance again to col-

lect Jonno from the emergency department and found him chatting to one of the doctors, having transferred their patient to the team in Resus.

'Maria's come through surgery,' he relayed. 'She's in ICU but it looks as if we got her here in time.'

'She's one of the lucky ones,' the doctor said. 'Good job, guys.'

Back on station, Jonno started quizzing her on whether she thought they could have done anything differently in their treatment of Maria, like doing something to try and lower her blood pressure? And why had he given her an anti-nausea drug?

'I'm guessing vomiting could have put additional pressure on a dissection and turned it into a full-on rupture? I don't know about the blood pressure management.' Brie held her hands up in surrender. 'I think my brain's fried. It's been quite a night.'

'Sorry.' Jonno's smile was apologetic. 'I've been acting like you're getting ready for sitting your critical care paramedic assessment. Not very fair, is it?'

'I loved it,' Brie assured him. 'I can't believe I'm lucky enough to be doing a few shifts with someone like you so I can learn so much. If I ever do get to be a critical care paramedic, I'll have you to thank for giving me a head start.'

'It's my pleasure,' Jonno said. 'It's the sort of thing that I love doing for a friend.' One side of his mouth curled up in what looked like a hopeful smile this time. 'We can be friends, yes?'

Brie felt her heart sinking. She wanted to be but it was impossible while she was keeping the truth from Jonno. She tried to smile back and hoped it would be enough of an answer.

It seemed to be. Jonno's smile widened. 'That's great. I'm heading off for a bit of rock climbing in Scotland with my mate, Max, tomorrow but I'll be back before you start your next shift. Dave tells me that Simon might be back on deck by then so I might not see so much of you. How 'bout I get your phone number and then I can ask you a favour. As, you know…' there was a sparkle in his eyes now that matched that smile '…a friend.'

'Sure.' Brie pulled out her phone and tapped the screen. 'Give me your number and I'll send you a text.'

She put the numbers in for a new contact and put a smiley face in the message line and hit the send arrow. As she put Jonno's name

in the contact details it felt oddly significant.
As if Jonno was officially part of her life now.

'I need a friend to help me with some paint-
ing if you have a bit of spare time when I'm
back,' Jonno was saying as she slipped her
phone back into her pocket. 'I'm not so bad
with a roller but I'm really hopeless with a
brush for doing the outlines.'

Brie didn't believe that for a minute but
she knew what the real request was here.
Jonno wanted to spend some time with her
away from work. Maybe he had more in mind
than getting some help with his renovation,
but that wasn't what was foremost in Brie's
thoughts right then.

This was exactly the opportunity she'd
been waiting for.

A private space, away from work, to tell
Jonno what he needed to know.

No excuses, this time. She would go to
Jonno's apartment and tell him about his son.
Because it was the right thing to do.

And because there was just the faintest
hope that he might not react the way Brie
feared. That she wasn't going to make his
life implode in what could be his worst night-
mare.

That, once Jonno got his head around it,

there was even a chance that they *could* be friends? That he could, somehow, be a part of his son's life without breaking his little heart?

CHAPTER FIVE

TEN O'CLOCK IN the morning seemed like the safest time possible to be alone with Jonno Morgan.

It was during daytime hours, which removed any romantic associations that could have come from candlelight or the moon. It wasn't lunchtime, which removed any incentive for alcohol to be offered at this time of day, and Brie was hardly dressed to impress. She was wearing her oldest tee shirt and a pair of dungarees that had splatters of paint all over them from being used for her own DIY decorating projects in the past.

Not that Brie was anticipating wielding a paintbrush once she had dropped that paternity bombshell onto Jonno. Unless he wanted to talk about it in detail, in which case, doing something at the same time could possibly defuse some of the inevitable tension?

What Brie hadn't bargained on, as she arrived to knock on the door of Jonno's apartment, were memories waiting to ambush her. The way she'd come down this path last time, with her hand lost in the grip of Jonno's. The way she'd held the cold bottle of champagne so he could find his keys and unlock the door. And the way he'd given up the search so that he could use both his hands to cradle Brie's face and kiss her for the very first time.

She also hadn't factored in that Jonno might also be wearing old, ragged, paint-spattered clothing. That his tee shirt had a ripped hem that revealed a triangle-shaped patch of his skin. That oh, so soft skin on his side, just above his hipbone and below his ribs. That his jeans looked a size too big and were hanging so low on his hips the waistband of his underwear could be seen. Or, heaven help her, he didn't look as if he'd shaved in several days and his hair certainly hadn't seen a brush in a while. There were even flecks of paint adorning those wild, black waves.

And the smile…

Jonno looked so happy. A smile that would be obliterated very soon, when he heard what Brie was about to say. The sooner the better, in fact, because she could feel her resolve ebbing away under the effect of a smile that advertised how delighted he was to see her.

Had he thought that she might change her mind and not turn up, given that her text response to his invitation had only said she'd do her best to come to help this morning if nothing got in the way?

She'd been giving herself an insurance policy, hadn't she, in case her nerves got the better of her?

'Hey…' she said by way of a greeting as Jonno opened the door.

'I'm so glad you're here,' he said. 'Please, come in…' He held the door open, but the gap for Brie to move past him was narrow enough for her to feel the heat of his body.

Oh, help…she hadn't expected that either. Or that she could be aware of the scent of him despite the paint fumes in the apartment and it was triggering an avalanche of memories she didn't dare acknowledge.

'I had to come,' she said, pulling in a determined new breath. 'There's something I really need to tell you, Jonno.'

'Me too,' Jonno said, pushing the front door closed. 'You were right.'

'What about?'

'Come and see…' He took hold of her hand as he caught up with her in the narrow hallway and pulled her to the door opposite the open-plan living area she was heading for.

Before she had time to even say another word, he was leading her through the door to the bedroom. 'The aubergine would have been a disaster.' He waved his free hand at a test pot sample he'd painted on the wall. 'But... what do you think of this? It's a half-shade of olive-green.'

'It's lovely. Good choice.' But Brie's gaze strayed from the pretty pale green as she tried to collect her thoughts and find a way to open the conversation she should have already had with Jonno. Years ago.

But she found herself staring at the wall beneath the window where there were still patches of wallpaper that needed stripping.

She could see one of those damned up-side-down pineapples. That avalanche of memories was coming for her. She could see it moving so fast, there was a layer of mist above it—one that already seemed to be making her brain feel foggy. Just what had that opening line been to tell Jonno that he had a son? In desperation, Brie jerked her gaze away from the pineapples. She turned away from them completely, only to find that she was not only standing too close to Jonno to allow for that turn to offer an escape route, she was also under a very intense gaze from a pair of dark, dark eyes.

Jonno wasn't smiling now. In fact, his face was more than serious. He almost looked... sad? Poignant, anyway. As if he was thinking of something bittersweet.

'Why did you run away while I was asleep that night, Brie?' he asked softly. 'You didn't even leave a note. Did I do something that upset you?'

'*No...*' Brie's eyes widened. How on earth could he be thinking that when every single thing he'd done that night had been beyond wonderful? 'It was nothing like that.'

'What was it, then? I've always wondered.'

'I...um... I was feeling a bit sick. I would have been so embarrassed if I'd thrown up in your apartment. I'd had way more to drink than I usually do.'

Jonno's face stilled. 'Is that what it is? Why you're keeping your distance? Did I take advantage of you?' His words were quiet. 'I could have stopped, you know. You only needed to say the word. But I thought you wanted it as much as I did.'

'I *did*...' Brie whispered. Dear Lord, she could remember the level of that desire so clearly. Probably because she could feel the tendrils of that need tying themselves in a knot again right now, deep in her belly.

You *do*...you mean. That little voice in the

back of her head was correcting her, even as she spoke. You still want it, you know you do. This is how you find out what's missing in your life and the fact that you want it *this* much is telling you how important it is.

She couldn't look away from Jonno's gaze but his silence was unnerving her. She had to break it.

'You've got some paint on your face.' Her voice sounded oddly raw. 'Right by the corner of your eye.'

'Oh?' Jonno lifted his hand and used his middle finger to brush at his skin.

'Not there. The other eye.'

He tried again but still missed the splash of paint and, without thinking, Brie lifted her hand and touched the paint that was crinkled by his smile lines. Jonno caught her wrist loosely with one hand as she touched his skin and he used his other hand to touch *her* face even though they both knew perfectly well that she didn't have any paint that needed wiping off.

His touch was feather-light but startling enough for Brie to have caught his gaze directly again. She could see the clear message that he would back off if she moved even a fraction away from that touch. He would drop his hand and that would be that. The music would be killed and the first steps of this dance would be the last.

But Brie didn't move away. As she closed her eyes she could feel herself leaning her cheek into the palm of Jonno's hand. And then she heard the way his breath came out with an undertone of sound that was exactly what she was feeling.

Raw need.

Pure desire.

Exactly the way this had started the first time.

Brie didn't open her eyes because she wanted to feel the heat of Jonno's lips taking her by surprise as they touched hers. She knew that heat would spark a reaction that she had no desire to dampen. She had to feel this again.

Just once...

He hadn't misremembered.

Or hyped up anything about that night with Brie into some kind of dream that had no basis in reality.

In actual fact, this new reality was better than anything Jonno had remembered. The sheer magnitude of the attraction that only built on itself from the first touch and *taste* of Brie's skin. The exquisite pain of slowing things down that pushed desire to limits he'd only ever discovered existed because of that night with this woman.

One kiss that led into another, deeper conversation between their lips and tongues. Questions that were instantly answered. Pleasure that was both given and taken in equal amounts. Buttons being undone, tee shirts being lifted for hands to find bare skin. It was a physical dance with a sense of urgency dampened only by the knowledge that if they went too fast this would all be over far too soon.

The bed that had been in this room the last time this had happened was long gone. Right now, the only furniture was a mattress on the floor that was covered with a drop sheet. The room smelled of fresh paint and, if they weren't careful, they might knock over a tin of pale, olive green liquid, but Jonno couldn't have cared less.

What he did care about was whether there was some reason why this shouldn't be happening at all.

'Do you want this?' he whispered against the side of Brie's neck as his fingers paused against her back, poised to unfasten the clasp of her bra. 'Is it okay?'

Her head tipped back to expose that vulnerable dip in her neck where Jonno could see how fast her heart was beating. 'I want it,' she murmured. 'Don't stop... *Please* don't stop...'

Desire kicked up several more notches. Who knew that had even been a possibility?

'Are you still on the pill?'

'*No*...' There was a note of something like anguish in Brie's tone. She must want this as much as he did if she felt like this at the prospect of having to stop.

'That's okay... I've got something...'

Of course he did. Tucked into a hidden pocket in his wallet. Jonno would never take risks with anything like birth control. And you never knew when you might meet an amazing woman who was happy to live in the moment and take pleasure in a one-off encounter of such an intimate nature.

This wasn't a one-off, of course, because they'd done it before. But that had been so long ago that it felt like it could be a first time with each delicious surprise of an unexpected touch...or lick. Then again, there was a feeling of safety. Of familiarity. Of knowing that this was even better than the first time because of that emotional umbrella that felt like trust.

He heard Brie cry out with the first stroke of his fingers and then again as he entered

a space that had haunted his dreams for so
many years. It was the sound of a woman in
ecstasy. A woman who'd just been given exactly what she'd needed the most. And then
he felt Brie's legs wrapping around his, the
pressure urging him on. It was *his* turn now.
She wanted to give him the same gift.

It was a long time before Jonno had any
vaguely coherent thoughts he could collect
but, gradually, despite the continued float-
ing sensation that was the aftermath of a release like no other, he became aware of the
warmth and shape of the woman he was holding gently in his arms and the rise and fall of
her breasts as her breathing slowed.

'You okay?' he queried softly. Jonno didn't
open his eyes because he didn't want to break
this spell.

'Yeah…' He could hear the smile in Brie's
voice. 'Never better.'

Jonno pulled her a little closer. He pressed
a slow kiss against the top of her head.

'You want to get up? Are you hungry?
Did you know I'm probably the world's best
cheese toastie maker?'

He loved the sound of Brie's laughter. 'No,
I did not know that.'

'Do you like cheese toasties?'

'Who doesn't?' But Brie snuggled closer.

'I don't want to get up just yet, though. Talk to me?'

'What about?'

'Anything... Everything...'

The warning bell sounding faintly in the background of Jonno's thoughts was enough to make him open his eyes and stare at the ceiling. He would never stay in one place long enough to talk about 'everything'. This was all about the sex. And friendship, if Brie could be one of those rare women who didn't expect it to automatically grow into something more. Or she didn't find a proper relationship where a close friendship with another man wasn't acceptable.

'You do know I'm not going to be around that long, don't you?' His words were quiet.

'I know.'

'And I don't believe in marriage. Or long-term relationships. I've never wanted my own family.'

Brie didn't say anything this time but Jonno could feel the shape of her body become more defined in his arms. Muscles had tensed and he knew he'd broken that blissful spell, but this was important. He couldn't let her think for a moment that this could be anything more than what it was, because that was the way people got badly hurt. He didn't usually go into details but Brie was different.

Because this wasn't the first time.

And Jonno was kind of hoping it might not be the last time.

'I grew up in what looked like the perfect family,' he told Brie slowly. 'From the outside. A successful father, a beautiful mother who devoted her life to charity work and helping less fortunate people. I got into a prestigious boarding school. I was the luckiest kid ever. Until I was about fifteen and it all fell apart in such spectacular fashion that there was no way I was ever going to believe in happy families again.'

'What happened?'

Jonno closed his eyes again. He let out his breath in a long sigh. He never talked about this but… Brie was different. And he wanted her to understand. So that she wouldn't get hurt. Or maybe it was so she would understand in case he'd hurt her somehow the first time they'd been together, without intending to.

'There was an accident,' he said. 'A nasty car crash. One of Bristol's leading philanthropists was driving. My mother was in the passenger seat. They were both killed instantly, and that was when the scandal broke.'

Brie was silent. Waiting…

'It turned out the guy was just the latest in a string of affairs my mother had been having throughout her entire marriage. She'd used this apartment to keep her liaisons private. Everyone who was anyone in Bristol seemed to be involved and everyone was shocked. My parents had presented the façade of a perfect marriage. My father would be there in his tuxedo at every glittering charity event and my mother, in one of her gorgeous ball-gowns, would be hanging onto his arm, playing the adoring wife. There were photoshoots at home occasionally and I'd be in the background somewhere—the perfect child of the perfect mother. It was all a total sham. Totally fake.'

Brie made a sound as if something hurt. He felt her fingers move against his arm as if she wanted him to know she was right there. On his side?

'It would have been awful enough to lose a parent,' she said softly. 'Without finding out any of that. Especially at that age, when it's enough of a challenge to figure out the world and where you fit into it.'

'I didn't fit,' Jonno said. 'Not for a very long time. I'd lost the mother I adored, but she wasn't who I thought she was. I felt cheated.

And angry. I used to go to friends' houses for school holidays, so I barely spoke to my father for years. He tried to tell me that he'd married my mother because she was pregnant and then he stayed with her because he didn't want to lose his son, but I was never going to forgive either of them. When I was eighteen I got access to what my mother had left me, which was this apartment and rather a lot of money, and it gave me an escape route. I told my father that I'd done a DNA test and he wasn't even related to me biologically. It didn't surprise him at all.'

He could feel the brush of Brie's hair against his skin as she shook her head in sympathy. Or disbelief, perhaps.

'So there you go. I was expected to follow in my father's footsteps and go to medical school but I took off. The money I inherited meant I could do whatever I wanted. I got a job as a ski instructor in the Swiss Alps and met people who introduced me to all sorts of adventure sports. And then I got involved in an accident up in the mountains and that was when I decided to train as a paramedic. The rest, as they say, is history. What goes around comes around. My mate Max and I got involved in a mountain rescue a couple of days ago up in the Cairngorms.'

Was Brie aware that he was deliberately changing the subject? If so, she didn't seem to mind.

'Really? What happened?'

'It was another group of rock climbers. They got caught in a rockfall and one guy got a nasty compound fracture of his femur. Luckily, I carry a good first aid kit so we could give some decent pain relief before we splinted his leg and carried him to a spot the helicopter could land.'

'Sounds like a mission.'

'It was. We had to give up our plan to tackle Squareface.'

'Squareface?'

'It's a nice, gnarly climb that we've had on the bucket list for a while now. Never mind… We've booked another couple of days up there next month and we'll have to do it then or the weather will get worse and too much rain makes it hard to get through the river, and who knows when we'd get another chance? Anyway… Max messaged me this morning to tell me there's a picture of us on the front page of half a dozen newspapers.'

Brie gave a huff of laughter. 'I always knew you were destined to be famous. Way back, when I kept hearing people talking about you even before I was the one who got to dispatch you the jobs where all hell was breaking loose.'

'Just the way I like things to be.' Jonno grinned. 'Living on the edge. Apart from the times I like things to be just…like this…' Jonno smiled, shifting her in his arms so that his lips could find hers. '*Exactly* like this…'

Oh, man…the way she could respond to what felt more like a thought than a physical touch was mind-blowing. It was no wonder he'd never been able to forget Brie Henderson. He'd never met someone who was so in tune with how he rolled. Who he was. A random thought that, if things had been different, Brie would be his perfect life partner drifted through Jonno's mind some time later, when he truly felt too exhausted to move. And then another thought pushed it out of the way.

'What was it?' he asked, his voice sleepy.

'What was what?'

'The thing that you said you had to tell me? The reason you came today?'

Brie's intake of breath a beat later was almost a gasp. 'Oh, my God…what time is it?'

Jonno reached for the watch he'd dropped beside the mattress. 'Just after half past two. Must be time for that toastie, huh?'

But Brie was already on her feet, pulling

on her underwear. 'I can't stay.' She reached for the paint-splattered tee shirt and pulled it over her head. 'I'm sorry but I've... I've got to be somewhere.'

'That was what you had to tell me?'

'No...not exactly...' Brie was halfway into her dungarees now and looking around for her shoes.

'But you can't stay,' Jonno finished for her. 'Are you running away from me, Brie? Again...?'

Brie froze, her shoes in her hands. She shook her head but she was looking wary again.

Guilty, even?

Yeah...he'd been right to feel that something didn't add up here. And maybe what he needed to do was back off. He didn't need, or want, to get involved in someone else's life to the extent that it interfered with his own life.

'It's no big deal,' he assured Brie. 'You go and do what you need to do.' He reached for his own scattered clothing. 'I got a bit distracted from the things I need to be doing myself.' He walked towards her, to drop a slow kiss onto her lips. Just to let her know there were no hard feelings, even if she *was* running away from him again.

She kissed him back. As if she simply couldn't help sinking into one final kiss.

And then she was gone.

CHAPTER SIX

SHE'D NEVER FELT like this.

Ever.

Brie arrived in the nick of time to collect Felix when his school day ended at three o'clock.

She'd never felt this guilty before. She'd thrown away the perfect opportunity to do what she knew she had to do, which was to tell Jonno that he had a son. But how could she when he'd opened up about some really traumatic things that had shaped him into the person he was today? Brie had a whole new understanding of made Jonno Morgan tick and her heart had gone out to that troubled teenager he'd once been. He'd felt betrayed by a mother he said he'd adored. He'd hated the man he'd thought was his father, who had contributed to the sham marriage they'd had. And what about his biological father that he hadn't mentioned? Did he feel as if he'd been betrayed by him as well? His family had clearly been a disaster he never wanted to repeat, so how could she have told him he was a father himself in that moment?

Okay...she could have told him as soon as she'd arrived at the apartment, which had been her absolute intention. But she'd been sucked back into the past, thanks to that damned wallpaper.

Taken back to a time in her life when everything was all about herself and there were still endless opportunities in her search for her place in the world and true happiness. To a time when dreams could actually come true and the man she'd hero-worshipped from afar had not only noticed that she existed but he'd *wanted* her.

Brie had been pulled back to that very brief window in time—the space of one night— when it had felt as if every bit of romantic nonsense she'd ever heard was actually true. That you could find 'the one' you were meant to be with. The person who could touch your soul at the same time as your body and that combination was so intense that you knew you could never, ever find it with anybody else.

Even another glimpse of that dream was something Brie had never thought she'd find and the temptation to actually *feel* it again had been totally irresistible. Just once.

And the result was that, yes, she felt more guilty than ever before. But she'd never felt this *happy* before either.

It felt a whole lot like being in love...

Which put Jonathon Morgan firmly amongst the people that Brie cared about.

The people that needed to be protected.

Feeling like she was protecting everyone involved made it easier not to let the feelings of guilt become overwhelming. This needed to be dealt with one step at a time and surely the fact a new, stronger connection was being forged between herself and Jonno was a step in the right direction? Laying the foundation for a future that all the people she cared about the most would be sharing to some extent?

Guilt versus happiness. Selfishness versus caring for others. Add them all together and the result was confusion.

It was doing Brie's head in, but she wasn't about to let Felix see the dark side of her thoughts. She took him and Dennis to the park after school because the sun was shining, and they were both in fits of laughter as they watched Dennis plough into drifts of autumn leaves and then pop out of the centre of the pile. She bought ice creams on the way home and had dinner ready for Elsie when she got home from a yoga class to get ready for a night shift on the paediatric ward.

It wasn't until Felix was tucked up in bed and Brie went to help her mother with the dishes that she found herself under her mother's watchful gaze.

'So it went well? Better than you expected?'

'Um…' Oh, wow… Brie dried a plate rather more thoroughly than it needed and turned away to put it in the cupboard. As close as she was to her mother, there were some things that weren't up for discussion and sex with Jonno was currently at the top of that list.

'You did tell him, didn't you?'

'Not exactly.'

'Oh… *Brie*…' Elsie sighed. 'Why not?'

'Because he told me that he doesn't believe in marriage or long-term relationships and he's never wanted a family of his own. He stopped believing in families at all after the horrible way his own family disintegrated when he was about fifteen. No more than a kid, really. He doesn't want anything to do with families, so it was hardly a good time to tell him he's got one of his own, was it?'

Elsie just shook her head.

'I feel like I know him a whole lot better than I did, Mum. It was the first time we've really talked, you know? He was trusting me with some pretty personal information. If I told him now, he might just take off and we'd never see him again.'

'You make it sound like he's going to do that anyway. What happened that was so terrible in his own family?'

It was Brie's turn to shake her head. It wasn't her story to share. 'He trusted me,' she repeated. 'And if I can prove that he *can* trust me, it could change everything. Oh… guess what?'

'What?'

'There's a photo of him in the paper today. I bought a copy when Felix and I had an ice cream on the way home from the park. Want to see what he looks like?'

'Of course.'

There was an undeniable feeling of pride as Brie showed her mother the picture of the hero paramedic who'd saved a man's leg, if not his life, in the mountains of Scotland.

Pride mixed with the memory of how it had felt lying in his arms today. Feeling his heart beating against her own. Feeling as if there was no other place in the universe that she could ever feel quite like this.

If Jonno was feeling anything like she was tonight, surely it *could* change everything?

Because it felt as if a few hours of being with Jonno was never going to be enough.

That even a lifetime might not be enough?

Yeah…this certainly felt an awful lot like being in love…

Elsie Henderson had a baby in her arms and she couldn't put him down.

If she did, his face would crumple and he'd start to whimper and she'd already spent too much of this night shift trying to get this miserable six-month-old baby boy called Tommy to settle enough to get some much-needed sleep.

She had been walking up and down the central corridor for some time now, talking to Tommy in the soft whisper that was apparently very soothing. Elsie had long since run out of things to say about the antics of all the animals crowding the brightly decorated walls of this paediatric ward and, a while ago, she'd started simply thinking out loud, finding something personally soothing about releasing thoughts that were starting to pile up enough to be concerning.

'So, you know what I think, Tommy? I think she's dating him. I *think*…she might have slept with him, though she's not telling me anything. She's got this… I don't know…

glow about her. And she's so happy. If I didn't know better I'd say she was head over heels in love...'

Elsie smiled down at Tommy as she shifted what was becoming quite a heavy weight in her arms.

'I'm not saying it's not good to be in love. Or happy, for that matter. We all want to be happy, and it's all we want for our children. And that's why I haven't said anything. The only thing I do know is that she hasn't told him yet and I'm not happy about it at all. Surely she could have found the right moment today? I get that it might spoil what could be happening between her and Jonno, but that's just selfish, isn't it? This has to be about what's right for Felix. And his daddy. Even if Brie is happier than I've ever seen her...'

Elsie let her breath out in a long sigh. Her arms were starting to ache and she needed to put Tommy down, or at least sit down herself for a while. One of those comfortable armchairs in the corner of the staffroom would be perfect. She walked past the central desk in the ward and another one of the night nurses looked up.

'Is that Tommy?'

Elsie nodded. 'He's finally asleep,' she said,

as quietly as she could. 'But I can't put him down without him waking up.'

'Don't put him down. I'll keep an eye on your other patients. It's only an hour or so before the day shift starts arriving and that wee guy should be due for some more pain-killers by then.'

Elsie carried on towards the staffroom but Tommy was moving his head and making little grunting noises as if he was thinking of waking up.

'Shh...' Elsie bounced him very gently in her arms. 'It's okay... Here we go, let's find that comfy chair.'

There were two armchairs on either side of the coffee table by the window, but one of them was already occupied. By someone she would never have expected to be using it, especially at this time of night. Elsie bit her lip as she eyed the other chair.

'I'm not in your way, am I? I can go...' The man hurriedly put the mug he was holding down on the table. Too hurriedly, because it tipped over to soak a section of a messy, well-read newspaper. He groaned as he grabbed the mug and it sounded as if this might be the final straw.

'Don't worry about it,' Elsie told him. 'That paper looks due to go into the recycle bin anyway.' She was watching his face and could see deep lines of fatigue around his eyes. 'And don't get up. Please. You look like you need a quiet space even more than Tommy and I do, Mr Morgan.'

'Please, call me Anthony...'

She smiled, liking his informality. 'I'm Elsie, I've just started recently on this ward. I've seen you around before, of course, but not usually at silly o'clock.'

The surgeon met her gaze for the first time. 'It has been rather a long night. I've been in PICU since midnight with a wee girl who looked like she might not make it. She had a fairly major surgery today and ran into problems with arrhythmias that put her into acute heart failure.'

'Oh... I'm sorry.' Elsie held his gaze for a heartbeat longer. She knew that Anthony Morgan had a reputation for being one of the best paediatric cardiac surgeons in the business but this was palpable evidence of how much he actually cared about his young patients and Elsie couldn't help but be seriously impressed. But then her eyes widened.

'It wasn't Victoria, was it? I knew she was having her surgery.'

Shutters came down that told Elsie he wasn't about to break rules concerning privacy and she had another very strong impression about this man. He could keep a secret for ever if he needed to.

'Sorry,' she said again. 'I shouldn't have asked. It's just that I spent some time talking to Vicky's mother the last time I was on duty. I'm helping to raise a grandson with spina bifida so we had a connection. And Vicky's just an adorable little girl. She gives the best cuddles in the world—just like my Felix.'

Those shutters in his eyes had been lifted in a slow blink. Anthony was even smiling. 'She's okay. She's a wee fighter. Her cardiologist has got her electrolyte balance sorted now, so she may well come onto the ward in the next day or two and you might be able to get another one of those cuddles. Is your grandson the same age?'

'No, he's six—a couple of years older. We've been through a few surgeries ourselves, but nothing as serious as an open-heart procedure.'

'I'm glad he hasn't needed it.' Anthony nodded but then stifled a yawn. 'I don't actually need to be here for Vicky any longer but if I went home I would no sooner get there than I'd have to turn around and fight my way through rush hour traffic to come back. I've got a full Theatre list this morning so I thought I'd put my feet up here instead. And have a strong coffee.' He glanced down at the empty mug in his hand. 'So much for that plan.'

Tommy seemed to be enjoying the sound of their voices. Elsie could feel him sink into deeper slumber as she took his weight on one arm. 'Here…give that to me.' She held her hand out for the mug. 'I'm well practised in making a coffee one-handed. Why don't you put the newspaper in the recycle bin by the fridge?'

'Sure.' Anthony started to gather up the sections of the paper.

'How do you take your coffee?'

'Black, thanks. No sugar.'

It was easy to pour coffee from the glass carafe that was part of the drip coffee percolator. Elsie took the mug back to Anthony, to find that he hadn't got very far with moving the coffee-splattered newspaper. He had it in his hand instead and was staring at the picture on the front page.

Elsie had seen that picture herself. A few days ago now. Because Brie had brought the paper home with her. After throwing away what must have been the best opportunity she could have had to tell him about his son.

'*Look, Mum,*' she'd said. '*That's Jonno. He*

and his friend were rock climbing in Scotland and they ended up rescuing this guy who'd broken his leg. I thought you might like to see what he looks like.'

Elsie had done more than simply admire the action shot of the paramedic with his grateful patient as he got loaded into a rescue helicopter. She'd cut the picture out and had it in safe keeping because one day—hopefully very soon—she would be able to give it to Felix. To put the first picture of his daddy on the wall, even?

Anthony didn't seem to notice Elsie putting the mug of coffee down beside him. Or that she was watching him as she sank into the other armchair, careful not to disturb Tommy. There was something about how still Anthony was that made the back of her neck prickle. Something that made those lines of weariness in his face look a lot more like…grief?

'Do you know him?' she asked softly. 'Is he a relative of yours?'

Anthony didn't seem to notice that it might be odd she could remember the surname of someone she'd seen in the caption of a newspaper image. He seemed lost in the photograph.

'Yeah…' The tone of just that one word was raw. It had an echo of fatigue that almost sounded like despair. 'Jonathon Morgan is my son.'

Elsie froze. Brie had been quite sure that Jonno was not related to this surgeon with the same surname.

He specifically said he had no family here...

But had that been the truth? What about what she'd said after she'd spent time with him the other day?

He stopped believing in families at all after the horrible way his own family disintegrated when he was about fifteen...

Anthony put the paper down. Then he closed his eyes and rubbed his forehead with his fingers. 'Sorry,' he murmured. 'Maybe the night's been longer than I realised. I'm quite sure you don't want to hear about my personal life.' He had a smile on his face as he opened his eyes but he didn't meet Elsie's gaze. 'Families, huh?' He reached for his coffee. 'They can be complicated, can't they?'

Elsie's sound of agreement was a little strangled. She was staring at him. He had no idea just how much more complicated his family might actually be.

Anthony Morgan was clearly well aware of the difficulties in his relationship with his son.

What he couldn't possibly know was that his son had a child he still didn't know he had.

That Anthony had a grandson he didn't know he had.

The weight of Elsie's concern about the way Brie was handling this whole situation had just become a whole heap bigger. As if he could sense the tension, Tommy woke up with a start and decided to let the world know that he was a long way from being happy.

Elsie got to her feet and excused herself as the baby's cries rapidly became ear-splitting. She needed to get Tommy back to his room so she could check on his nappy and see whether he was due for a feed or that his medication dose could be brought forward if necessary. She could feel the misery of this howling infant settling around her own heart as she carried him and it was morphing with that concern about Brie.

How was she going to tell her daughter that Jonno had lied to her? That Felix's father might not be trustworthy? That there was now another grandparent in the picture, and didn't Anthony Morgan have the right to know about Felix as well?

Families were complicated, all right.

Elsie had no idea where she could even

start to try and sort the unexpected issues that were landing on her own family but one thing was clear.

As much as Elsie adored her daughter, Felix was the person who mattered the most right now. Whatever she decided to do, or not do, could affect her grandson's whole future.

CHAPTER SEVEN

BRIE HENDERSON MIGHT be thirty-two years
old and a highly competent single mother but
she knew she might have made a mistake in
not paying enough attention to the words of
wisdom from her own mother.

Elsie had warned her that the longer she left
it, the harder it was going to be to tell Jonno.

And Brie's intimate reunion at Jonno's
apartment had just made it a whole lot harder.

When he smiled at her like *that* it was impossible to think of anything other than the
way it felt to have Jonno touching her. There
were moments when she could feel a glance
from him burning through her clothes from
the other side of the station staffroom. Even
the sound of his voice, or his laughter, could
send a delicious shiver down her spine and
she had to be careful not to let eye contact
linger long enough for it to be blatantly obvious that they were more than colleagues.

It was just as well they weren't working together.

Brie's original crew partner, Simon, was back at work but, in the wake of his recent head injury, he was being sheltered as much as possible from any stressful situations that might be too much of a challenge so the calls they were being dispatched to were low acuity. Not that Brie was about to complain because this was the kind of experience she needed and Simon was happy to take the role of a mentor and let her take the lead.

She assessed a twelve-year-old boy who'd fallen off his bike on the way to school and had a Colles fracture of his wrist and Simon was pleased with the way she splinted the injury, remembering to put something soft for the boy's fingers to curl around and keep the fracture stable. She dealt with a known epileptic who'd had a seizure in a video arcade but refused transport to hospital by the time Simon and Brie arrived on scene. He confessed he hadn't been taking his medication recently and he also knew that the flashing lights of the arcade games were a trigger for him. He apologised for wasting their time and Brie assured him that this was what they were here for. She made him promise to take more responsibility for his own health from now on.

'It could have been worse, you know? What if you'd been riding your bicycle and you'd fallen off in the middle of traffic?'

There was a pregnant woman who thought she might be in labour and wanted a ride to the hospital and a very elderly gentleman whom they found sitting in an armchair with a bag beside him. Brie could see the neatly folded pyjamas and a plastic bag with a toothbrush and toothpaste on top of it. It sounded as if Clive had also googled and then memorised all the classic symptoms of a heart attack.

'I've got terrible central chest pain, love,' he said to Brie. 'And it's radiating to my left arm and my jaw. I feel lightheaded. Faint, even…and I'm really short of breath.' He took a couple of quick gasps.

'Have you been sick at all?'

'Not yet. But I feel like I could be. Any minute.'

'How bad is the pain? On a scale of zero to ten, with zero being no pain and ten being the worst you can imagine?'

'Oh…' Clive screwed his eyes shut and pressed a fist to his chest. 'Ten…' He opened his eyes and smiled bravely at Brie. 'Maybe just a nine. I'm pretty tough, you know?'

Brie smiled back. 'I know. But it's a bit scary if you're feeling sick and there's no one around. Do you live alone here?'

Faded blue eyes had a sparkle that looked like imminent tears as Clive nodded. This was a lonely old man and, if they weren't needed urgently elsewhere, what was the harm in spending some time to give him some attention and reassurance? They had to take any report of symptoms like this seriously anyway, even if Clive didn't look as if he was at all unwell or suffering from severe pain.

'I'm going to give you the full work up,' Brie told him. 'I'll take your pulse and your blood pressure and look at the oxygen saturation in your blood. We'll do a twelve lead ECG as well. Have you had one of those before?'

'I have indeed.' Clive lay back in his armchair. 'You do whatever you need to do, darling. I have complete faith in you.'

So did Simon as their shift drew to a close. He had let her take the lead in every callout, including the last one, which had been a lights and siren response to a medical alarm.

'You're already way more confident in your

assessments,' he told her as they headed back to station. 'And you just got that IV line in on your first attempt.'

'My hands were a bit shaky,' Brie admitted. 'I've never had to deal with a case of hypoglycaemia that severe. I thought she was dead when we first walked in. And her veins were so hard to find.'

'Giving the IV ten percent dextrose is a bit of magic, isn't it?' Simon was smiling. 'I know it's not as exciting as being out as crew on one of the Echo trucks but it's always been a favourite job for me. Especially like Glenys today, when they wake up like a light switch going on.'

Brie laughed. 'She was so with it. The way her eyes popped open and she said, "Oh, no… I've had a hypo, haven't I?" She was so annoyed with herself.'

'At least she had the good sense to activate her alarm when she felt the first symptoms. She could have been in real trouble if she hadn't.' Simon was rubbing his forehead.

'You've got a headache again, haven't you?'

'Yeah… I'm glad it's nearly home time.' His eyes narrowed as they slowed down. 'What's with this traffic?'

'I don't know. Oh, wait… I can see some beacons behind us.' Brie pulled the ambulance closer to the side of the road as a police car pushed its way through the traffic. Moments later, the flashing lights of another emergency vehicle appeared in the rear-view mirror and, at the same time, the radio in the ambulance crackled into life.

'Unit Four-Zero-Three, how do you read?'

Brie pushed the talk button. 'Loud and clear, Control.'

'Your location is Queen's Road, correct?'

'Roger that.'

'Please proceed to the intersection of Queen's Road and Charlotte Street. There's a car that's gone through the window of a coffee shop. Details coming through. You're backing up Echo One.'

The vehicle with its flashing blue lights and the siren sounding was passing them as Brie activated the lights on the ambulance and pulled out to follow it. She knew who was driving the rapid response vehicle. Her heart rate would have picked up even if this didn't appear to be the most exciting call she and Simon had had all day.

The fact that she was about to be in the same place at the same time as Jonno was just as exciting as any major trauma case could be. Brie hit the air horn as another car tried to pull out in front of them. She wasn't about to let anything get in her way or slow her down.

The scene was a mess.

A car was half in the café and half on the footpath with broken pieces of the outdoor tables and chairs scattered around. Police officers were trying to direct traffic and clear space and spectators, which was not an easy task because of the busy junction nearby.

Jonno was first on scene for medical assistance and left the beacons on his vehicle flashing as he got out, looking for whoever had already taken charge of the scene. He could see a fire engine approaching from one side and an ambulance was arriving from the same direction he'd come from. A police officer standing at the rear of the crashed car waved him over.

'Was anybody sitting outside?' Jonno asked.

'Fortunately not,' the police officer responded. 'And there's only a couple of people with minor injuries inside. They had time to jump out of the way, apparently. The driver of the car is elderly. Seems like they were intending to park but hit the accelerator instead of the brake. Unless there's something medical going on. He's refusing to get out of his car. There's a doctor in there talking to him.'

'Okay… I'll take a quick look but it sounds as if I'm not really needed here.'

A glance over his shoulder showed Jonno that the ambulance had found a space to park and it sounded as if their crew would be easily able to handle whatever was happening inside the café. When he saw it was Brie getting out of the driver's seat in the ambulance, however, Jonno found himself dismissing his plan of making himself instantly available for another call. When his gaze caught hers, even across a gap as big as this, in the middle of a chaotic accident scene, he was aware of what could be seen as a rather unprofessional desire to stay here.

But, on the other hand, he was nearing the end of his shift so there would be another rapid response vehicle available very soon and maybe he needed to take a bit more time to assess this situation. Driving through a shop window had the potential to be quite a serious mechanism of injury, didn't it?

And…what if Brie needed his help? Her crew partner was looking a bit pale himself. Had he come back to work too soon after getting that nasty concussion? Jonno wasn't about to have Brie left to deal with everything on her own, like she had when he'd found her looking after that woman who'd nearly been murdered by her husband.

So he walked into the café with Brie. Side by side. He could see the back of the man, presumably the doctor the police officer had told him about. Had he happened to be in here for a coffee, perhaps? They weren't far away from St Nick's children's hospital here. Whoever he was, the man was crouched beside the open driver's door, his hand on the wrist of the elderly driver, who was still gripping his steering wheel and staring straight ahead. A table lay on its side nearby, along with a splintered chair and broken crockery on a carpet of shattered glass.

There were several other people in the café's interior, possibly because the crashed car and all the emergency personnel were blocking the café doors. A man in a chef's apron had a bloodstained tea towel wrapped around someone's arm. Two middle-aged women were still sitting at a table with plates of cake in front of them, staring wide-eyed at what was going on, and there was another woman in the corner closest to the door they had just come through. Beside the only intact part of the front windows of the café. She had streaks of grey in her hair and an alarmed expression, but what Jonno was most aware of was that she was holding onto the handles of a wheelchair that had a small boy sitting in it. A small boy who was also wide-eyed. Even more so when he saw Jonno and Brie walk inside. The astonished expression on his face now was almost comical.

'Mumma!' he shouted. 'Look, Nana…it's *Mumma*.'

Confused, Jonno turned to see that Brie now looked far paler than Simon had.

She looked beyond shocked, in fact, as she moved towards them.

'Mum…what on earth are you doing here? Are you hurt?' Brie dropped to crouch in front of the wheelchair. 'Felix? Are you okay, darling?'

The small boy was climbing out of his wheelchair and Jonno could see the braces he was wearing on his lower legs. From the corner of his eye he could see the man who'd been talking to the driver of the car getting to his feet but he wasn't ready to talk to him yet. Because he was watching the little boy wrap his arms around Brie's neck and the way she got to her feet with him clinging to her like a little monkey.

Holding him the way a mother would hold her child so that she could reassure him. Or reassure herself that he wasn't hurt?

So Brie did have a child, not just a dog.

Had she lied to him about being single, as well?

Distracted far more than he should ever have been in a professional situation, Jonno tried to centre himself. He turned away from watching Brie cuddling her son to talk to the doctor who had already assessed the driver who'd come through the wall of this café.

But the distraction of seeing Brie with her child was nothing compared to the shock that Jonno was now faced with. He was standing within touching distance of a man he hadn't seen for a very long time, but it wasn't long enough.

Because this was a man he'd believed he never wanted to see again.

But he'd never realised he would feel this… *pull*…towards this man if he did see him again.

His father…

His only family…

For a heartbeat the two men stared at each other. And then Anthony Morgan's gaze went past him, towards Brie and her mother and the kid, and Jonno knew instantly that this couldn't be simply a coincidence. There was a link here and it had to do with Brie.

And his connection to Brie.

He could feel the axis of his entire world shifting beneath his feet. Kind of like the way it had when he'd been hardly more than a kid himself and he'd been told his mother was dead. When he'd found out that the world as he'd known it hadn't actually existed.

But it made absolutely no sense that it could be happening again.

He turned back to his father. 'What the *hell* is going on here? No…' He held up his hand as he saw the older man about to respond. 'It can wait. I've got patients who need attention. Simon?' He turned his back on his father. 'Could you give me a hand here, please?'

'What *is* going on, Mum?' Brie echoed Jonno's angry question as she put Felix back into his wheelchair. 'Who is that man? Someone said he's a doctor, so what's so wrong about him helping the driver of that car?'

'Nothing.' Elsie shook her head. 'He *is* a doctor. He's Anthony Morgan.'

Part of Brie's brain was trying to join dots so that she could make sense of this, as another part reminded her at the same time that it was her job to find any people other than the elderly car driver who might need medical attention. Like that man with the tea towel wrapped around his arm. Yet another part was noticing the way her mother was swallowing hard, as if she had something difficult to say. Felix didn't seem to be aware of any sudden tension. He was watching the actions of police officers and firemen again with total fascination.

'He's also Jonno's father.' Elsie was avoiding Brie's gaze now, her voice deliberately casual and low enough not to attract Felix's attention. 'He...um...wanted to meet his grandson.'

Those dots didn't just connect. They smashed into each other.

'How *could* you?' There was only one way that this stranger could have learned of any connection to Jonathon Morgan's son and Brie felt utterly betrayed, but this wasn't the time or place to confront her mother. 'Take Felix home, please.'

'But...'

'*Now*...' Brie turned away, managing to find a smile for Felix. 'I'll see you soon,' she promised. 'But I've got work I have to do right now.' She stepped towards the man with the tea towel. 'Can I see your arm?' she asked. 'How did your injury happen?'

'Bit of flying glass,' he said. 'I pulled it out but it wouldn't stop bleeding.'

As Brie began unwrapping the bloodstained cloth she glanced up to see the doctor—Jonno's *father*—moving past her, leaving Jonno and Simon to reassess the man in the car. He wasn't looking at her. Anthony Morgan's gaze was on her mother.

'I'm so sorry,' she heard Elsie say to him. 'We shouldn't have come here.'

'I'm glad we did.' Anthony Morgan sounded remarkably calm, Brie thought. There was a warmth to his tone as well that made her question the impression Jonno had given her that he wasn't a nice man. 'But I do think it's time we left. Let me help you get Felix back to your car.'

The laceration beneath the tea towel was a clean cut that was only oozing a small amount of blood now. Brie found a sterile dressing in her kit and a bandage to hold it in place.

'You're going to need a couple of stitches,' she advised. 'Have you got someone who can take you to your GP or the emergency department?'

He nodded. 'My girlfriend's over there.' He shook his head. 'We only came in for a coffee to takeout. Who knew something like this could happen?'

Brie wound the bandage around his arm swiftly. 'You were lucky you weren't standing any closer to the window.'

There were fire service personnel working with police officers as they assessed what needed to be done to remove the car and make the scene safe. One officer was talking to Jonno and others were helping to get the dazed-looking elderly man out of the driver's seat. Simon had hold of his arm.

'Just watch your feet, Mr Baxter,' he said. 'There's all sorts of broken stuff and I don't want you tripping up. We've just got to get out of the door and into the ambulance so we can take you to hospital for a proper checkup.' He turned his head, looking for Brie. 'You good to go?' he asked. 'Is there anyone else that needs us?'

'All good,' she responded. 'I'll just pack up my kit.' She gathered up the packaging from the dressing and bandage and stuffed it into her pocket before standing up again, with her backpack in her hands.

Only to find that Jonno was standing right in front of her. His face was pale, which made his eyes look even darker.

Even angrier…

'Did you know about this?' His voice was low. Dangerously quiet. 'Why *my* father and *your* mother were meeting?'

'*No*… I had no idea.'

'But you know *why*, don't you?'

Brie had to nod. She'd never felt this miserable in her life. She knew she had only seconds before she had to walk out of this café and finish the job she was responsible for. Time had run out. These few seconds were her last opportunity to tell the truth.

'My mother obviously thought your father had the right to meet my son...' However impossible it felt, Brie had to hold Jonno's gaze. She could see that Jonno knew what she was about to say but he wasn't going to make it any easier for her.

And why should he?

Her voice was no more than a ragged whisper as she finished her sentence. '...because you're Felix's father.'

Yep... Jonno had already guessed the truth and yet he'd managed to do his job without letting the bombshell interfere in any discernible fashion. Brie needed to channel that focus. She had an elderly patient who might not be seriously injured or unwell but he was probably already in the back of her ambulance and it was time to transport him to hospital.

But she couldn't break that eye contact quite yet. She knew Jonno had something he wanted to say and, however painful it might be, she owed it to him to let him say it.

It turned out to be more painful than she'd expected.

'I didn't think you were like *them*,' he said, his words dripping ice. 'But you're just the same, aren't you? You've been lying to me ever since I met you.'

CHAPTER EIGHT

'ECHO ONE, HOW do you read?'

'Echo One, reading you loud and clear.'

'Priority One call. Unwitnessed cardiac arrest of unknown duration. Private house. No bystander CPR underway. Police have been informed. Address should be on your screen now.'

Jonno flicked on his beacons and activated the siren, although, given the details he'd just received, it was unlikely that rushing to this scene would be of any benefit to the victim. His role was more likely to be that of being able to pronounce someone dead so that the police and coroner could take over but he was grateful for the automatic priority of the call.

He needed the buzz of the adrenaline rush that, even after so many years, still came from the sound and lights of a life-threatening emergency. From having to drive fast and think even faster so that he could anticipate and avoid hazards. This feeling was a drug and the effect that Jonno was most grateful for right now was that it made it impossible to think about anything else.

He reached the address within three minutes, well before any police were expected, but he knew that the scene of a sudden death was unlikely to be high on their priority list unless there were indications that it hadn't been natural. Jonno had to get there as quickly as possible, however. Just in case there was a chance it wasn't too late.

Jonno could sense that it was too late the moment he stepped through the front door to the house that had been left wide open. It wasn't simply the sound of a man sobbing, it was the oddly empty feeling in this house that he instinctively knew only came from being near someone who had no flicker of life left in their body.

The man was sitting at the table in his kitchen, a phone lying beside him, his face in his hands. His body was shaking with the effort to control his sobs when he looked up to see Jonno enter the room and he pointed to another door.

'She's in there… She said she felt tired and went to lie down…hours ago…' He pulled in a ragged breath. 'I thought she was just asleep...'

'Stay here for a minute. I'll be back...'

Jonno put his kit and the defibrillator down as he entered the bedroom because it was obvious as he approached the bed that the woman was deceased and there was no point in beginning a resuscitation. Her eyes were open and staring, her jaw drooping and he could see a bloodless pallor to her face and lips. He knew he would find her skin cool to the touch and her pupils fixed and dilated when he shone his penlight torch into her eyes. He still needed to observe her for long enough to be absolutely sure and Jonno put his stethoscope to her unmoving chest to listen for any sounds of life.

His protocol called for an ECG to be performed to demonstrate no cardiac activity but there was something more important to take care of first. Jonno went back to the kitchen and crouched so that he was at eye level with the grieving man.

'I'm so sorry for your loss,' he said quietly. 'Is there someone I can call to be with you?'

'My son's on his way.' The man rubbed at his dripping nose and sniffed loudly.

'My name's Jonno. I'll be with you until your son arrives but there are a few things

I need to do for...?' He raised his eyebrows. 'I'm really sorry, I wasn't told the name of your...wife, is it?'

He nodded. 'Margaret. But everyone calls her Peggy. We've been married for more than fifty years...'

'That's a long time.' Jonno smiled. 'And you are?'

'Trevor.'

'And Peggy wasn't feeling well today?'

'I thought she was fine. Just a bit tired...'

'Does she have any medical problems she was being treated for?'

'Oh, yes...she's had trouble with her heart for a long time now. And her blood pressure. Her breathing wasn't so great either, but she was doing well. We just celebrated her birthday last week. She's only seventy-three...' Trevor dissolved into tears again.

Jonno straightened, putting his hand on Trevor's shoulder. 'I'm going to put the kettle on,' he told him. 'And I'll be back to make you a cuppa. I've got a couple of things I need to do to tick the boxes on some paperwork, but after that would you like to come and sit with Peggy?'

The sound of Trevor's grief followed Jonno back into the bedroom. Any buzz of the adrenaline rush of getting to this scene had completely worn off now and, if anything, Jonno was feeling worse than he had before this call.

And that had been quite bad enough.

It was two days since he'd walked out of that café with an anger building to rival the worst of those teenage years when he'd felt betrayed by the people who should have cared about him the most. An anger that burned so brightly it was easy to channel it into action, focusing intently on his work and attacking all the remaining renovation work he could do himself out of work hours. Lack of sleep as he kept himself busy enough not to have to think about things had, no doubt, contributed to the weariness that was weighing him down now. Along with a disappointment that was so deep it actually hurt to breathe if he let himself think about it.

Jonno gently closed Peggy's eyes before opening the pockets on the defibrillator to find the electrodes he needed to stick to her skin to take his ECG recording. He found himself murmuring an apology as he pulled back the duvet and then lifted Peggy's clothing, treating her as respectfully as he would have if she had still been alive.

With all the electrodes in place, he turned on the defibrillator and watched as any artifact on the screen settled into the expected flat line. He pushed a button and the paper trace began to emerge, capturing the lack of any cardiac activity. He let it run for a few seconds and then stopped the trace, ripping off the recording so that he could attach it to the paperwork he needed to do.

He stared at that flat line for a long moment. Because it felt like a reflection of how he was feeling himself?

As if something had died?

But it had died a very long time ago, hadn't it? Why was it that the moment he'd recognised his father he'd become aware of this dark space in his heart? A family-shaped hole that he'd been living with for more than half his life, so it should have been filled by now with the satisfaction of his chosen career and the adrenaline-fuelled hobbies that were the focus of his free time.

He couldn't still love his father enough for this to be hurtful all over again, could he? Or had his anger diminished over the years enough to leave something exposed, but because he'd turned his back on it so long ago he hadn't seen it?

Jonno took a minute to get the room ready for Trevor to come back in to be with his wife. He tucked the duvet around Peggy's body. He closed the curtains and turned on a soft bed-side lamp. He put a chair beside the bed and then took one of Peggy's hands to lay on top of the duvet, so it could be held by grieving relatives.

It was then he noticed how beautifully manicured her nails were. Perfect ovals with a glossy red polish on them. She had a large diamond ring on her finger and there was something about that sparkle and those nails that took Jonno back in time with a jarring sensation. If Peggy's hand had a few more diamond rings on it, and a few less wrinkles, it would look exactly like his mother's hand had looked the last time he'd seen it.

Oh, man...that emotional hole was getting darker. Deeper. Jonno needed to get out of this room and do something that would distract him. The interruption of the middle-aged police officer who put his head around the door in that moment was more than welcome.

'Need any help?' he asked.

'I'm all done,' Jonno responded with a shake of his head.

'Nothing untoward?'

'No.' He hadn't noticed any red flags, like any sign of a struggle or evidence of drugs or alcohol being consumed. 'And there's a history of various medical issues. 'I'll be able to get out of the way as soon I've finished the paperwork.'

He'd be able to find something new to focus on, as well. Hopefully a complicated medical crisis that would allow nothing from his personal life to even enter his head. Because there was something even worse than having been reminded of a long-ago betrayal.

It was having history repeating itself.

But why had he expected anything to be different?

Jonno scribbled notes on the forms that needed filling and signed his name. He stapled the ECG trace to the back of the certificate and left a copy with the police officers present. Trevor's son and daughter-in-law had arrived and it was time Jonno left the family to have some time with their loved one before the next steps in the process had to occur.

He strapped the defibrillator back into its slot and shut the side hatch of his vehicle. Getting into the driver's seat, he was about to advise the control room of his availability but, instead, found himself closing his eyes and pulling in one of those unexpectedly painful breaths.

He had expected something different because he had *trusted* Brie.

He'd let her touch a part of his heart that he hadn't realised wasn't protected enough any more.

So now he felt betrayed all over again.

Because he'd felt closer to her than he'd allowed himself to be with any woman. With any person, come to that, after learning that his parents' marriage and, by association, their love for him, had been nothing more than a pretence.

He'd never felt like that about any woman.

He'd been in love with her, dammit.

She had been lying all along, but this time he couldn't run from the truth. He couldn't turn his back on people and places in order to shield himself.

He had a child.

A son. A small boy called Felix. And, if that wasn't enough to turn his entire world upside down, he had a child with special needs that made him even more vulnerable.

A child who had existed for years, but he'd never been told about him.

It was unforgivable. But Jonno wasn't about to walk away.

That would be more than unforgivable. It would be utterly unacceptable.

Letting his breath out in a sigh, Jonno reached for his phone and opened a contact he had resisted deleting in those first hours when he'd been so angry with Brie. He tapped in a text message.

We need to talk. And then I want to meet my son properly.

They met at Sugar Loaf Beach on the Severn Estuary.

Brie had suggested it because it gave her an excuse to take Dennis with her and she had a feeling she might need the comfort of her dog's company. Going to the beach was his favourite thing in the world, which also meant that at least one of them would be happy.

Jonno certainly wasn't. The look in his eyes as Brie walked towards him felt like a physical blow.

He hated her, didn't he?

And she couldn't blame him.

He barely made eye contact before leaning down to pat the dog's curly hair. 'So...this is Dennis?' His tone was polite. Cold.

Brie nodded and then realised Jonno wasn't about to look at her again so she cleared her throat. 'Yes... I hope you don't mind that I brought him. It's not often he gets to go to the beach.'

'I haven't been here since I was about Dennis's age.' Jonno tilted his head.

'Really? But you grew up in Bristol, like me, didn't you? These are our closest beaches.'

'I lived in Leigh Woods, which was the perfect place to grow up in with the forests and mountain bike trails to play in. For me, going to the beach meant a trip to Spain or the Maldives with my mother. My father could never get away from work, apparently, but, oddly enough, my mother would usually find a friend of hers who happened to be on holiday at the same time. In the same place. Always a male friend, of course—on holiday alone.'

Brie said nothing. Was he deliberately reminding her of that happy family image that had been contrived for public consumption? The lies he'd grown up with? That he considered her to be 'one of them'?

She wasn't. Deep down, she'd only ever wanted to be completely honest with Jonno. She'd been too shy in the beginning, given up too easily along the way and, most recently, too afraid to risk damaging the lives of the people she loved the most. Or too selfish, because she'd wanted that small piece of the fantasy back?

Jonno wasn't looking at her. He seemed

to be staring at the coast of Wales across the calm waters of the Severn estuary.

'Let's walk, shall we?' His tone was clipped. He didn't really want to be here, did he? He didn't want to have had his life tipped upside down.

Brie let Dennis off the lead and he raced ahead of them to get to the pebble beach that they appeared to have to themselves, which made the silence between them even more noticeable. Brie found a stick to throw and Dennis barked joyously as he chased it into the water. Then he found a seagull to chase instead and ran in circles as it flew overhead. The silence was feeling awkward now so Brie gathered her courage.

'I'm sorry,' she said.

'What for?' Jonno's words were still terse. 'That you got pregnant or that you got found out for lying for so long?'

'I'm not sorry I got pregnant.' Brie's response was swift. 'Felix is the best thing that's ever happened in my life.'

Apart from you, she added silently. *And the way you made me feel...*

'So...you lied to me about being on the pill? You *wanted* to get pregnant?'

'*No!*' The accusation was an insult. 'I'd never do something like that. I told you I'd left because I felt sick. I threw up, off and on, all day. I didn't miss any pills—it just didn't occur to me that it might have messed with my contraception.' Brie could feel her anger ebbing. She couldn't blame Jonno for thinking along those lines. 'I'm sorry that you found out the way you did,' she added. 'I didn't lie, exactly, but I should have told you sooner...'

Jonno gave a huff of unamused laughter. 'You think? Oh, right...maybe seven or so years ago?'

'I tried every way I could to contact you,' Brie said quietly. 'But it was weeks after you'd left. Your phone was disconnected. You never responded when I tried to message you on social media. Nobody knew where you were.'

'So you just gave up?'

'It was during those weeks I found out that the baby I was carrying had spina bifida.' Brie's tone changed. She might deserve Jonno's anger but she wasn't the person he thought she was. She hadn't set out to lie to him. 'My priorities kind of changed at that point.'

That silenced him. Brie walked ahead and found another stick to throw for Dennis. Then she turned.

'I never expected to see you again,' she

said. 'But when I'd had a bit of time to get used to you turning up out of blue like that, I did try to tell you—the day I came to your apartment.'

She could hear the echo of what she'd said to him then, in spite of the background shriek of the seagulls. She knew Jonno could hear it as well.

'I had to come... There's something I really need to tell you, Jonno...'

They both knew why she hadn't ended up telling him that day.

'You could have told me well before then. Like when I asked you if you had any kids.'

'Oh...yeah... Right after you'd been telling me how thankful you were that you didn't have any dependants? How much you'd hate to have a wife or kids that might stop you doing all the crazy, dangerous things you love so much? How do you think that made me feel?' Brie's voice hitched. 'I was still trying to get my head around it myself. How was I going to tell my son that his daddy was back in town but might not want to have anything to do with him because he had better things to do with his time? That he wasn't even planning to be around long, anyway. He was going to get rid of the last tie he had here and then he'd be gone again. For ever. Probably on the other side of the world in Australia or New Zealand.'

'I said those things because I didn't *know*,' Jonno countered. 'Do you really think I'm someone who'd walk away from a responsibility like having a child? That I wouldn't *care*?'

Brie swallowed hard. Of course she didn't. She found herself blinking back tears. 'I couldn't put your name on the birth certificate officially,' she said softly. 'But I wrote it on the back. Maybe I was hoping that one day Felix would be able to find you.'

Oh…*dammit*…

Maybe Jonno had wanted to hang onto his anger because it was easier than feeling *this*…

That, perhaps, he was the one in the wrong. That he'd gone off on his great adventures and deliberately cut all contact with the people he'd left behind. That Brie had had something so massive to face—not only single parenthood but knowing that her baby was facing physical challenges that could make life so much harder. That he had been careful to make it clear that he would never be interested in long-term relationships or having a family of his own. How thankful he was, in fact, that he didn't have any kids.

That he'd lied to *her* about not having any other ties in Bristol other than that apartment.

He knew Brie was covering up the fact that she was crying by throwing sticks for the dog. He saw her brush tears away as she stooped to pick up the stick and this had to be the worst feeling of all. Wanting to be able to comfort Brie and knowing that it simply wasn't possible. That he could do nothing to change everything she'd gone through so far and that they now had to sort out changes that were going to be life-changing for everybody concerned.

There was a large driftwood log on the beach just ahead of them.

'Come and sit down for a bit,' he called to Brie.

She turned her head and Jonno's heart broke a little at the pain he could see in her eyes. He remembered how he'd seen the wariness in her face when he'd landed back in her life. Fear, even? And he remembered the look of joy on that little boy's face as he'd reached up his arms to his beloved mumma. His son was very much loved—*genuinely* loved, unlike he had been himself—and there

was a big part of Jonno that was very grateful for that.

'Please...' he added. 'I want to hear about
it all. Right from the start...'

CHAPTER NINE

How was it possible to feel this close to someone yet, at the same time, to feel further apart than ever before?

Seven years was a lot of time to catch up on but it was such a relief for Brie to be able to be completely honest with Jonno that the words just tumbled out. She did start right at the beginning, apart from skipping over how that single night with Jonno had been a dream come true because this wasn't about *them* any longer.

Whatever might or might not have been simmering between Jonno and herself had become irrelevant because Brie knew it was dead in the water as far as Jonno was concerned. He had dismissed her as being 'just like *them*' which, presumably, meant his parents? Because they hadn't been honest. Because he'd seen his whole family as a sham.

So Brie was being completely honest. She

did start right at the beginning as far as Felix
was concerned, by telling him how shocked
she'd been to find herself pregnant. And that
she'd been even more upset to learn that there
was something wrong with her growing baby.

'I was about twenty weeks along when I
got the results of the second trimester alpha-
fetoprotein test that were elevated. Then the
roller coaster began with seeing all the specialists and having an MRI and the advanced
ultrasound tests. And, after I'd seen him on
the scans so clearly, they still gave me the op-
tion of ending the pregnancy...' Brie couldn't
stop fresh tears from rolling down her face.
'But it only made me want to protect him
even more... That was when they told me
about the possibility of having surgery before he was even born. That they could open
me up and then put the spinal cord back into
the spinal canal and close the tissue and skin
around it to protect it from exposure to the
amniotic fluid. It wasn't happening in the UK
then so I would have to travel to the States or
Switzerland or Belgium but it would be very
expensive and there were so many risks. He
could have been born prematurely. Or died.
I can only ever have a baby by Caesarean
because of uterine scarring.' Brie let out her
breath in a huff that was almost laughter. 'Not

that I'm ever planning to have another baby. But when they told me that foetal surgery can prevent the most severe brain malformations and mean that a child might be able to walk independently, I had to give him that chance, even though the risks were terrifying.'

She told him how it had turned their lives upside down to travel to Switzerland and have meetings with a huge team of prenatal specialists and social workers and psychologists. That she'd had to stay in the hospital for a week after the surgery and then have weeks more bed rest nearby before they'd let her go home, as long as she could travel to London every week for monitoring, and the focus on the baby she was carrying had only become more intense after he was born by elective Caesarean at thirty-seven weeks and needed more surgery in his first few days in the world.

Her voice wobbled as she told him it had become even harder when he was old enough to understand what was going to happen when he'd needed a shunt put in and corrective surgery on his feet, but she could smile with genuine happiness as she shared moments of joy at the milestones her brave little boy was determined to meet. There was laughter, even, as she answered Jonno's query of what he was like.

'I barely saw him at the café but I could see how close he is to you. How much he loves you—and your mum.'

'Felix loves everybody in his life and everybody adores him. He's such a...*happy* kid, I guess. Even when things are difficult or something hurts he can still find something to smile about. It's like he can find joy in thin air and then make it grow enough to share it without even trying. The world's a better place because Felix is in it.' Brie's smile seemed misty but then laughter bubbled. 'He learned to blow raspberries when he was a tiny baby and it made him laugh every single time. Then he discovered he could do a whale spout with a mouth full of water—in the physiotherapy pool—and that was the funniest thing ever. He still does it in the bath sometimes and it still makes us laugh.' She finished with a shrug. 'What can I say? He loves life. He's just the best kid in the world. It's partly how I chose his name because Felix means happy. And lucky. But I'm even luckier—that he's mine...'

Brie wrapped her arms around herself, feeling suddenly chilled from sitting here for so long. Or maybe it was something else that gave her that sudden shiver.

'I'd protect him with my life,' she said quietly. 'And I'm not going to let him be hurt, if there's any way I can help it. I don't want him to know that you're his father and get attached if you're just going to disappear on your next adventure and make him feel like he's not... I don't know, good enough to hang around for or something...'

'I'm not going to disappear.'

'You're going to stay in Bristol? For ever?'

'I don't know.' Jonno met her gaze directly and there was a new connection there that had absolutely nothing to do with any physical attraction. This was about honesty. About a very different kind of trust. 'I do know I won't make any promises I'm not going to keep. And I will promise that I won't do anything that could hurt Felix.'

Brie closed her eyes as she nodded slowly. She badly needed to believe that.

'Thank you for talking to me,' Jonno said.

'Thank you for listening.'

Jonno had listened to her story with what felt like compassion. He had seen her tears and her smiles. He'd reached down once or twice to pat Dennis, who'd curled up, finally tired out, by their feet but he hadn't touched

Brie. He hadn't held her gaze long enough for it to be anything more than you might do in polite conversation.

They were close enough to be talking about their son.

But distant enough to make physical contact unthinkable.

Brie looked down at the gap between them on the log. Only a matter of inches but it felt like miles. Whatever had happened between them since Jonno had been back in town was over but she wasn't even going to think about how much that hurt.

'I need you to do something else for me too, Brie.'

The sound of her name on his lips was bittersweet. It made her look up instantly to catch his gaze.

'I want to meet him. I get that it's too soon to tell him the truth, but I want to spend some time with him. Somewhere that you think will be safe.'

Brie nodded again. She'd already thought about this. About how she could still protect Felix when it happened.

'Why don't you come to his next riding class? There are lots of volunteers that help out at the RDA so it won't seem like anything out of the ordinary.'

For Felix, anyway. It would be huge for Brie but she knew it was going to be even bigger for Jonno. If he, as a parent, was going to feel even a fraction of how she felt about Felix, he had every reason to feel nervous about it, so she offered him a smile that felt almost shy.

'You'll love it,' she said. 'It's great fun and, like I said, he's the best kid in the whole world.'

'Have you had much to do with ponies?'

Jonno smiled at Kate, the woman in charge of this session at the RDA facilities. 'I worked in Mongolia for quite a while, for an adventure tourism company that took people on horseback through the desert or out onto the Steppes.'

'Wow…' Kate's eyes widened.

Jonno thought he heard Brie mutter something like *Of course you did…* which sounded rather like some kind of reprimand. An unjustified one because he hadn't done anything wrong. Not intentionally, anyway.

'I took part in the endurance charity challenge ride once,' Jonno added. 'The Gobi Gallop? We covered seven hundred kilometres in ten days.'

Kate was shaking her head. 'Well, all you

need to do here is walk on one side of Bonnie—the pony Felix is riding. His mum can walk on the other side and I'll take the lead rein. You're just an insurance policy in case Felix loses his balance.' One of the helpers getting Felix onto the pony waved in their direction. 'Looks like he's ready to go.'

'This is Jonno.' Brie's voice sounded a little tight as they took their positions on either side of Bonnie. 'He's going to help us today, okay?'

On top of the small pony, Felix was at the same level as Jonno. He eyed him up and then beamed at this new person in his life. 'I'm a 'questrian,' he told Jonno. 'I'm going to go in the Paralympics when I'm big.'

'That's very cool.' Jonno had to clear his throat and find a suitably impressed smile but there was something making his chest feel oddly tight.

That smile. That instant willingness to accept someone new in his life along with the sparkle in this little boy's eyes was sucking him in.

They were brown eyes. Dark brown eyes. Just like his own.

Oh, man… This felt so weird. He'd been around hundreds of kids in his lifetime. He'd taken care of them as patients and had always

felt the need to do everything he could to care
for such vulnerable little humans. He knew
the joy of winning a battle to save a small
life and he also knew the trauma and grief
of losing one.

But he'd never felt quite like this. As if
this bright, happy little boy was gripping his
heart as tightly as the reins he was clutching
in his hands.

Felix squeaked with excitement as Kate
clicked her tongue and encouraged Bonnie
to start walking and the sound made Jonno's
smile stretch into a grin. But then he caught
Brie's glance across the pony's back and suddenly he had to blink away an unexpected
moisture in his eyes.

'Can you make Bonnie turn right?' Kate
asked as they reached one end of the sawdust-
covered arena. 'Do you remember which rein
you use, Felix?'

'*This* one.' Felix lifted his right arm, with
the rein hanging in a very loose loop, but
Bonnie obligingly turned towards the right.
Felix tilted his head, trying to stay upright in
the saddle but look down at his mother at the
same time. 'Did you see me, Mumma? I did
it. All by myself.'

'You did, darling. I'm very proud of you.'

That tightness was there again. Good

grief...was this pride that Jonno was feeling as well? Like a parent might feel?

'I can ride all by myself,' Felix announced a few minutes later as they came to the other end of the covered arena and completed a turn to the left. 'Can I go faster now, Kate?'

Kate caught Brie's glance. 'Maybe we could try trotting just a couple of steps for the first time? What do you think, Mum? Are we ready?'

Brie looked across at Jonno, a question in her eyes.

'I've got this side covered,' he said. He did. If Felix got bounced out of the saddle he'd catch him in a heartbeat. He had the feeling it wouldn't be necessary, mind you.

'Hang onto the handle on the front of your saddle,' Kate told Felix. 'Don't worry about your reins this time.' She took hold of Bonnie's bridle and patted the pony's shaggy black neck. 'And...away we go...trot on, Bonnie...'

Bonnie appeared to understand the verbal instruction and broke into a gentle trot. Felix bounced up and down in the saddle and then lost his grip on the handle, but perhaps Bonnie felt him lose his balance because she slowed back to a walk at precisely the same moment. After teetering wildly enough for

Brie to reach towards him but not quite grab him, Felix anchored himself again by catching the handle attached to the pommel. Jonno could hear him pull in some air and it was only then that Jonno realised he'd been holding his own breath since Felix had started this first attempt at a faster pace.

His son's face was glowing with a mixture of astonishment, pride and sheer excitement. '*Again…*' he commanded. 'I want to do it again.'

Jonno could feel Brie's gaze on him again but he couldn't turn to meet it. Not until he'd blinked a few times, anyway.

Yeah…this was pride, all right. And something a whole lot bigger. Possibly the biggest feeling he'd ever had?

Jonno was looking a bit shellshocked, Brie thought as she fastened the buckle on Felix's car seat and closed the door.

'He'll probably fall asleep before we even get home,' she said. 'That was a lot of excitement for one day.' She swallowed hard. 'And he didn't even know the half of it, did he?'

'Trotting for the first time was quite enough excitement for one day. He did so well, didn't he?'

'He did.' Brie knew her smile was one of deep pride. 'But you know...he is a 'questrian.'

Jonno didn't laugh. His smile was decidedly crooked, in fact. 'I felt so proud of him. Is that weird?'

Brie shook her head. It wasn't weird at all, although she hadn't expected he might feel such an instant bond with Felix. She wasn't exactly sure how she felt about it either. Her smile was rapidly vanishing.

'I'd better get him home,' she said. She turned away with a sigh.

'You okay?' Jonno's voice was quiet behind her. 'I know that this can't be easy for you either, but this was a brilliant idea and... I really appreciate the way you've made it easy for me to meet Felix.'

Brie turned back. 'It's not you,' she told him. 'Things are a bit...um...strained at home, I guess. I still can't believe that my mother thought it was acceptable to tell your father he has a grandchild before you even knew about it yourself.' She shook her head. 'We're not exactly happy with each other right now. I'm even thinking it might be time for me and Felix to find a place of our own.'

'I'm sorry to hear that...'

'She thinks I should have told you sooner. And she still thinks Anthony had the right to know, even though he isn't actually related to you, biologically.'

'Who told you that?'

'Seems like my mother and your father had a big heart-to-heart. She's a paediatric nurse and they met at St Nick's. It was that photo of you in the newspaper from that rescue in the Cairngorms that started it. He told her that you were his son. It was only after she told him about Felix a few days later that he said he wasn't actually your real father, but my mother said that of course he was.' Brie's shrug was apologetic. She was embarrassed by her mother's interference but she also didn't want to lose the new honesty that she had with Jonno and he deserved to know what was being said behind his back. 'She said he was the man who'd brought you up. And when she asked if Anthony would still like to meet Felix, he just nodded. She said she thought he had tears in his eyes.'

Jonno's lips were a thin line. 'At least you and your mum are still talking. I'm sure you'll sort it out. It's so many years since I spoke to my father, I wouldn't know where to start. Or even if I want to.'

He turned away from her and Brie could see that Felix was watching him through the window as he waited patiently for his mum to get into the car. She saw him smile at Jonno and, when Jonno smiled back without hesitation, her heart melted a little. With relief? Or something a whole lot deeper?

'Maybe you should talk to him,' she said quietly. 'Mum said that when he saw your picture in the paper he looked really sad. And when he talked about you later he was obviously very proud of you.'

This time, when Jonno turned away, he started walking away from her. Increasing this new distance which made it feel as if she was being shut out of a big part of Jonno's life.

Of being allowed to connect to the person he really was?

'Thanks again,' he said. 'I'll see you at work tomorrow, yeah? Maybe we can find time to talk about what we're going to do next.'

'Sure. I'll make a copy of his timetable for you so you can see what you might be able to come along to. There's a movement and music class coming up if you're free that day?'

'Sounds fun. Let me know where and when.' Jonno turned his head to catch her gaze. 'And one other thing, Brie...'

'Yes?' A splash of hope blossomed somewhere deep inside Brie's chest and grew astonishingly quickly. Was Jonno going to say something that might suggest he didn't hate her? That there was hope they could not only navigate this new space they found themselves in but that it could connect them even more significantly on a personal level?

But there was no warmth in Jonno's eyes. 'If you've got any copies of the medical records for Felix, I'd really like to see them.'

Hope was being pulled out by the roots to die a quick death, which was remarkably painful.

'I've kept everything,' Brie told him. 'I'll bring the folder into work tomorrow.'

Brie hadn't been exaggerating about keeping everything.

And it was astonishing how images and words on paper could tell a story that let you get to know someone on a completely new level.

Not just his son, although he could read between the lines of the medical reports he was browsing in his late evenings and actually feel the courage of a small boy recovering from surgeries or that determination to learn to walk unaided. He could also feel the love of a mother who'd kept the first ultrasound images of her baby, the first recording of his heart, X-ray images from before and after surgeries, even the first prescription for glasses that would help him see clearly. There was a note scribbled on the form to say that Felix had his heart set on the brightest red frames if possible.

He must have had several changes of prescription and frame size since then but his colour preference hadn't changed. He'd been wearing his bright red glasses at his riding lesson and he was wearing them again when Jonno arrived in time for the music and movement class he'd been invited to attend and went to sit with Brie and the other parents to watch.

But Felix was waving at him. 'I want Jonno to do it with me,' he called. 'Please...?'

Jonno could sense that Brie was a little taken aback by the plea and was about to say he was happier to simply watch but then Brie caught his glance.

'There are quite a few kids who like their parents to do the class with them,' she said.

How could Jonno say no to that? Felix might not know he was a parent—*his* parent—but he wanted Jonno to do this class with him and that was even more impossible to say no to. And it *was* fun. There were songs to be sung and instruments to be played. Felix chose a tambourine. Jonno decided to shake some maracas and earned a grin from a man who was helping his son bang a drum.

Felix led the way with Jonno close behind when the teacher sent them all over the hall with suggestions of how they could move to a frequently changing variety of music.

'Be an aeroplane,' she called. 'Or a butterfly. And now you're all robots...'

Finally, before they were all too tired, there was an enormous rainbow-coloured parachute and everybody—parents and children—got to hold onto the edges and lift it up and down to make it float. It was hard to try and do it in time to the music but it didn't matter and if someone lost their grip there were shouts of laughter as they tried to catch it again.

Jonno helped the teacher fold the parachute while Brie got Felix into his coat and settled into his wheelchair for a rest.

'I haven't seen you before,' the teacher said. 'Are you Felix's dad?'

'I am,' Jonno told her. 'And you'll be seeing me again soon, I hope. I haven't had so much fun in ages.'

'Felix obviously loved having you here,' she said with a smile. 'He always looks like such a happy kid but today he was just glowing.'

Yeah... Jonno could feel that glow himself.

Maybe that was why he suggested they went to a nearby fast-food restaurant for an early dinner instead of saying goodbye outside the hall. They ate hamburgers and he made Felix laugh by showing him how to put French fries under his top lip so they stuck out like walrus tusks. He expected Brie to tell them to stop playing with the food when she shook her head but she was smiling.

'Can I go in the playground, Mumma?' Felix asked.

'It's time we went home,' she said. 'Dennis will be wanting *his* dinner.'

'But I want to show Jonno how I can climb in the tunnel,' Felix protested. 'And go down the slide by myself.'

'Maybe just for a few minutes. Jonno might need to go soon too.' Brie caught Jonno's gaze and there was a question there. Maybe it was simply a small question about whether he wanted to spend a little extra time with Felix today. But it felt like a much bigger question, about how much of the rest of his life did he want to devote to his son and that was…disturbing?

Because it was…huge, that was what it was.

If he wanted to be the kind of father he hadn't had himself—one that was available and interested and truly present in his life, it represented a very different future to anything Jonno had planned. Or wanted…?

Felix was climbing out of his wheelchair.

'Wait for me, buddy.' It was a relief to have an excuse to turn away from Brie and the prospect of confirming a commitment he was still coming to terms with. 'Am I allowed to go on the slide as well?'

CHAPTER TEN

THE SMELL OF lasagne was enough to bring tears to Brie's eyes when she stepped through the back door into the kitchen. She couldn't remember when her mother had last cooked her favourite meal.

Oh, yeah...that's right. It had been the day that Jonno had crashed back into her life. Her first day on shift as a qualified paramedic and that dramatic job that she would never forget.

Brie was never going to forget today's last job either. And it seemed that the horror of it was still written on her face because Elsie went pale herself.

'What's happened?'

Elsie was on her feet as she spoke, pulling Brie into her arms in the same way she had always done as a completely automatic response to her daughter needing comfort, but it had been a long time since Brie had felt an embrace like this. Too long.

'Are you okay, love?'

Brie let herself sink into that familiar warmth for a heartbeat longer. With the background of the aroma of the hot food in this small room, it felt as if she were being transported back to her childhood. To a time when the world was a safe place because she and her mum had each other.

'Not really,' Brie admitted as she pulled away. 'I'll tell you about it in a minute. I... I just need to give Felix a kiss. I'm guessing he's asleep by now?'

'I hope so.' Elsie bit her lip. 'He was a bit quiet this evening. He didn't eat much of his dinner either, and he loves lasagne as much as you do.'

'Was he upset that I was going to be so late?'

'I think it's more likely he's just coming down with a cold or something.'

Brie was already on her way upstairs. Her little boy was sound asleep. His breathing was regular and his skin felt a normal temperature when she touched her lips to his forehead gently enough not to wake him but he stirred and opened his eyes. Then he smiled at her. His words were slurred by being sleep-drunk.

'Love you, Mumma...'

'Love you more, Bubba.' Brie brushed a

lock of hair off his forehead and kissed him again. 'Sweet dreams...' She glanced up at the star-spangled ceiling of his bedroom. 'Did you make a wish?'

Felix nodded. 'Special wish...' he mumbled.

'What did you wish for?'

But he was asleep again and this time Brie wasn't going to disturb him.

Elsie had poured a glass of wine for her when she got back to the kitchen. 'I know it's a day shift for you tomorrow but...'

But she was a mother and she'd needed to do something to comfort her child? Brie understood completely. 'Thanks, Mum.'

'You hungry?'

'Not really.' But she knew that the food was another peace offering. 'Maybe later? It smells amazing.'

Brie took a sip of her wine. 'I'm sorry I'm so late. My station manager, Dave, wanted me to have a chat to a counsellor before I went home.'

Elsie had worked in the medical world long enough to know why that might have been important. 'Oh, no... Was it a child?'

'Just a baby.' Brie nodded. 'Three months old. Got put down for an afternoon nap and never woke up.' She picked up her glass and took a long sip. 'She was still warm,' she said softly. 'But we were way too late. We did everything we could. We had critical care backup and continued CPR all the way to the hospital. *They* did everything they could but...' Brie closed her eyes. 'She was so tiny, Mum, on that hospital bed. And her mother was so utterly broken...'

'Oh, love...' Elsie put her hand over Brie's and squeezed it. 'There's nothing worse. I'm so sorry...'

'It's part of the job, as you know all too well. You had to cope with that little girl dying on *your* watch not that long ago. And, as the counsellor told me, knowing how that mother was feeling was part of what's going to make me very good at my job, but I've got to protect myself as well or I'll burn out fast. He told me to go home and cuddle my son and take comfort in being with my family.' Brie blinked back new tears. 'I'm sorry, Mum.'

'Whatever for?'

'I've been horrible to you lately. We've hardly been talking.'

'That was my fault, not yours. I shouldn't have put my oar in and told Anthony about Felix. I forced you into a conversation you weren't ready for.'

'And I should have had that conversation earlier. I didn't because...' Brie stopped abruptly. She could say she'd been trying to protect Felix, and that was absolutely true, but there was a selfish aspect about it that she wasn't proud of. She'd wanted to step back into that fantasy, hadn't she? *So* much...

Elsie's tone was tentative. 'Because there's something happening between you two?'

Brie shrugged. 'Not now. I'm not sure there ever was...on Jonno's side, anyway.' She slid a sideways glance at her mother. 'How did you guess? I never said anything.'

'I could feel it. And I knew there had to have been something there in the first place or you would never have gone to bed with him. Are you still in love with him?'

Brie avoided a direct response. 'I feel the same way I've always felt about him. It's never been anything...real.'

The silence that fell between them threatened to push them apart again.

'Was it Jonno that backed you up today for that horrible job?' Elsie asked.

'No. He'd taken the afternoon off. There's a rumour that he went to a job interview at the air rescue base.'

'For a permanent job? Here, in Bristol?'

'Maybe.' Brie's glass was half empty now. 'He hasn't said anything to me about it.'

'But he might be planning to stay.' Elsie sounded hopeful. 'He gets on well with Felix, doesn't he?'

'He's brilliant with kids. And Felix thinks the sun shines out of him.'

'He certainly talks about him a lot. On the way home from school today, I got to hear all about the ponies that Jonno galloped across the desert. Are you... I mean, have you talked about when you'll...' Elsie bit her lip. 'No... I'm not going to ask. I'm keeping my oars firmly in my own boat from now on.'

'When we'll tell him?' Brie finished her wine as well as her mother's query. 'Soon. As soon as I can be sure Jonno's not going to do a disappearing act. He's still planning to sell his apartment. It's on the market already, in fact. He said he can't wait to get rid of it.'

And Brie hadn't been able to stop herself wondering if that had anything to do with the reminders of what had happened between them in that bedroom? Because he still hadn't forgiven her for what he saw as dishonesty? They were still navigating this new space, connected by parenthood but with spiky boundaries around everything they had shared in the past.

'But he might be applying for a job here,' Elsie said. 'And he seems to want to spend more time with Felix. How did the dance class go yesterday?'

Brie finally found herself smiling again as the trauma of her day began to fade. While this new space she was in with Jonno felt fragile and restricted, there were still moments of unexpected joy to be found.

'Jonno joined in the dancing like it was his favourite thing ever,' she told Elsie. 'Then we went out for hamburgers and Jonno showed Felix how to make walrus tusks with his fries. They were both laughing so hard they couldn't eat them.'

Elsie was smiling too. 'Speaking of eating...are you at all hungry yet?'

'Do you know, I think I am... Have you had *your* dinner?'

'I was waiting for you...'

Brie let her breath out in a sigh, relieved that the recent tension between them seemed to have evaporated. Home was definitely the place she'd needed to be this evening. It was even better to remember the pleasure of seeing Jonno interact with his son yesterday and...maybe hope was contagious because Brie found herself wondering if that rumour had been true and Jonno was thinking of taking a permanent job in Bristol.

That could change everything.

It would mean Jonno would become a real part of their lives.

Of *her* life.

Could she cope with that? Knowing that the man she was in love with was only there because of her child? *Their* child?

Yeah…if he was going to bring more joy and love into the life of that precious child, Brie would welcome his presence. Because that was what mothers did—they put their children first.

'You must be starving.' Brie smiled at Elsie. 'Let's eat…'

The offer that came through on the apartment within just a few days of it going on the market was a bit of a shock, to be honest.

It wasn't that Jonno couldn't deal with another life change. He was, after all, an expert in tipping his life upside down and then shaking it to see what fell out and whether he was tempted to give something completely different a good try—preferably something that had a bit of danger or unpredictability about it.

Oddly, however, in these last few weeks, it was predictability that he was placing the most value on. Like knowing the times he was going to spend with Felix in his activities outside school hours, which meant he was getting to know his son and getting used to the shock of discovering that he was a father.

The email from the estate agent that pinged into his phone as he arrived at work a day or two later, with a better-than-expected offer from a client already on her books that she had taken to view the property before its first open home, should have been a pleasant surprise but Jonno wasn't sure how he felt about it yet. Because it meant that decisions needed to be made a lot sooner than he'd thought he would have to make them, even if he could push the settlement date out by a month or two.

Big decisions might need even longer than that to be sure about, though. Like where he was going to live. Should he buy a kid-friendly sort of house for when the stage might be reached that his son would want to have a sleepover at his dad's house? The kind of house he'd grown up in himself, with room to play hide and seek inside and a garden that was big enough to kick a football around in? Near that wonderful park with the forests and bike trails or close to the sea in a suburb near Portishead or Sugar Loaf Beach?

It was something he'd been putting off even thinking about for precisely this reason. Because it made him think about what had been good about his own childhood, and that made him think about his father and he wasn't ready to think about that when he was still getting used to being a father himself. Despite Brie's advice to talk to him which kept replaying itself in the back of his mind, Jonno didn't feel remotely ready to talk to his father.

It was all too soon. Jonno was still processing the information in his son's extensive medical records, learning about every surgery he'd ever had and those still to come. He still hadn't come to the end of the folder, in fact, because Brie had included copies of school reports and dental examinations in the meticulous range of documents she had collected. He was still reading and absorbing every summary of outpatient clinic visits to his neurosurgeon and orthopaedic surgeon and urologist over the years.

Jonno hadn't even had any time alone with Felix yet. How could he, when the boy hadn't yet been told that Jonno was his father? Brie was, understandably, very protective and that made Jonno suddenly wonder whether she would let Felix stay in this hypothetical house by himself with his father or would she want to have a sleepover as well?

Oh, man... No. He had to stamp on that line of thought hard. Getting that close to Brie wasn't going to happen again. This was more than complicated enough as it was. Having been so determined not to allow history to repeat itself that he had avoided any long-term relationships himself, here he was on the cusp of committing to the longest term one imaginable—that of a parent and child. Not only that, it would also be a commitment to the mother of that child—the only woman Jonno had ever trusted enough for her to get past the protection that had been in place around his heart.

He had trusted her enough to feel betrayed by her not telling him sooner about Felix.

Enough to feel as if something important had died. The potential future with the only woman he'd ever fallen in love with, perhaps?

How was he going to be able to make this work so that he didn't end up as distant as his own father had been when it was this complicated and there were the kind of huge emotions he'd been so careful to steer clear of?

Like trust.

And love.

Jonno felt a familiar urge to escape. To go and do something a bit dangerous that didn't allow for anything but complete focus if you wanted to stay alive. Like hang-gliding. Or rock climbing. He made a mental note to call his mate, Max, later today and check that their trip to Scotland was still on.

The day shift crews were checking over their vehicles as he walked through the garage and seeing Simon carrying a defibrillator towards an ambulance sent his thoughts straight back to Brie. She was probably in the back of that ambulance right now, making sure they weren't missing any supplies that might be vital today. That firm tug, somewhere deep in his gut, that made it irresistible to go and put his head around the open back doors of the vehicle to say hello was a warning he shouldn't ignore.

It should, in fact, be pushing him towards another big decision that was now looming as well—whether he wanted to accept the offer of a permanent job with the air rescue base that he'd received after Max had persuaded him to go and do that interview yesterday afternoon. If he was going to stay in Bristol, would it be better if he and Brie were working out of different bases to keep their professional and personal lives as separate as possible?

'You looking for Brie?' Simon caught up

with Jonno before he reached the ambulance. 'She's not here. I'm going solo for the day.'

'What? Where is she?'

'She called in sick.'

Okay, that was another warning, that kick in his gut at the idea of Brie being unwell.

'It's not her,' Simon added. 'Sounds like her kid is a bit off-colour so she's keeping him out of school today.'

The idea of Felix being unwell was turning that sensation in his gut into an unpleasant knot. 'What's wrong with him?'

'No idea. Not much, I don't think, but Dave said he thought it was probably a good idea if Brie had a day off. After yesterday…'

'Yesterday?' Jonno could feel his frown deepening. 'Have I missed something?'

'Last job of the shift was a three-month-old baby that was DOA. SIDS. Don't know about you but I sure remember my first one. Brie coped amazingly well on scene, but afterwards she looked like she'd been hit by a truck.'

Jonno *felt* like he'd been hit by a truck. He was pulling out his phone as he walked away from Simon. He had fifteen minutes before his shift was due to start so he could ring Brie and check that she was okay. That Felix was okay.

Except he didn't get the chance. He could see the station manager, Dave, striding into the garage.

'Jonno—good, I was hoping you were in early. Are you able to take a priority call right now?'

'Ah…sure…' Jonno turned to walk to where the rapid response vehicle was parked but he fired a sharp glance at Dave. This was a really odd way to be responded to a call.

Dave knew why he was getting the look. 'Control gave me a heads-up,' he said quietly. 'It's Brie's house.'

Jonno felt a chill run down his spine. He pulled open the driver's door. 'Do you know any details?'

'Yes. It's her kid. Six-year-old boy who has spina bifida. Apparently he's having, or has just had, a seizure. I'll send Simon as backup in case you need to transport.'

'You might need to get someone in to cover the rest of my shift too,' Jonno said. 'It's not just Brie's kid. It's mine.'

Dave's jaw dropped. 'I can't send you for first response. You're too involved.'

'Don't try and stop me,' Jonno warned. 'I need to be there. Now…'

'Then I'm coming with you.' Dave pulled

open the passenger's door of the rapid response vehicle.

Jonno was already in the driver's seat. He could see the suggested route on the GPS on his dashboard screen as soon as he turned the ignition key. He put his safety belt on as he waited impatiently for the huge garage doors to rumble up far enough to get out without catching the beacons he already had flashing on the roof of his vehicle. He flicked on the siren as the barrier arm in the car park swung up to let him into the traffic.

And then he put his foot down. It didn't matter how quickly he was going to be able to get there.

It was still going to take too long.

CHAPTER ELEVEN

DESPITE MOVING SO quickly as he led the way into Brie's house, Jonno found himself hyperaware of tiny details.

Like this neat little suburban house where his son lived with his mother and grandmother. An ordinary little three-bedroom, end-of-terrace house that reminded him of... Oh, yeah...the surprising location of the violent situation he'd discovered the day he'd answered the emergency Code Black alert to find Brie on her first shift as a paramedic, working alone as she tried to manage a woman about to go into a respiratory arrest.

Was she alone again right now? Trying to keep her son alive?

Their son...

He found her in the kitchen. On the floor. Holding Felix in her arms. He could see the little boy was not conscious. He could see the terrible fear in Brie's eyes.

He knew what he should be doing. He had to find out whether Felix was at all responsive. Was he simply asleep and easily rousable, in a postictal state after a seizure and sleepy and confused, or was he unconscious for a more sinister reason? He needed to check his heart and respiratory rate, listen for any sounds of an impaired airway and check the colour and temperature of his skin at the same time.

But, for one horrible, frozen moment, as he saw how limp Felix was and how pale his face was, it occurred to him that his son could be dead.

It was a good thing Dave had come with him on that wild ride to get here as fast as possible and Simon would not be far behind with his well-equipped ambulance, but the quick glance from Dave with his silent query about whether he needed to step back was enough for Jonno to take control of his emotional reaction. He owed it to Brie to do whatever he could for their child. He owed it to Felix to do his best to protect him.

Brie let him take Felix out of her arms and put him down gently on the floor.

'Hey, buddy…what's happening?'

There was no response to Jonno's voice. Or to the pinch on his earlobe that should have elicited a response to pain. And he wasn't moving at all.

He broke his initial visual assessment of Felix to catch Brie's gaze for a heartbeat. 'What happened exactly?'

'I'd taken Dennis outside. I heard a thump and I came in to find Felix on the floor in a full tonic-clonic seizure. I'm not sure if he fell off the chair or just knocked it over.'

Jonno lifted an eyelid and shone his pen-light torch, relieved to see that Felix's pupil sizes were equal and that they reacted to the light with normal speed.

'Have you noticed any sign of a head injury?'

'No.'

Jonno was feeling the small skull beneath his fingers, anyway. He couldn't feel any lumps or bumps and there was no sign of any bleeding. 'And he was unwell enough this morning for you to decide to keep him home from school? Was his behaviour unusual in any way?'

'He was slow to wake up, which isn't like him, but I guess it started last night. Mum said he didn't want his dinner. She thought he might be coming down with a cold and he had a bit of a temperature this morning. He was rubbing his eyes, which usually means he's got a headache, so I gave him some paracetamol. It was Dennis who was really behaving oddly. He refused to leave Felix and go outside to pee. That's why I took him out...'

From the corner of his eye, Jonno could see Dennis huddled in the corner, under the table. The little dog looked as frightened as Brie.

'Has Felix vomited at all? Complained of anything hurting?'

'No...' Brie's breath hitched. 'But he never complains. Not unless things get really bad.'

Jonno was watching the way Felix was breathing, looking for signs that he was in difficulty. The rate of breathing was higher than normal but he couldn't hear any sounds of airway obstruction. He lifted the little boy's clothing to look for retraction of the muscles between his ribs but he needed to check his skin for any evidence of a rash that might indicate a medical emergency like meningitis and he also wanted to stick some ECG electrodes in place. An oxygen saturation probe completely covered one of Felix's tiny fingers but Jonno was happy to see that his cardiac rhythm and oxygen levels were okay.

'How long did the seizure last for?'

'I'm not sure. It felt like ages but it was

probably only about two minutes. I was already ringing triple nine as it stopped.'

'Has he woken up at all since?'

Brie shook her head.

'Has he had seizures before?' Dave had a paediatric oxygen mask in his hand as he connected the tubing to the cylinder he'd brought in.

'No, never.'

'He's had borderline increased cranial pressure in the past, though, hasn't he?' Part of Jonno's brain was lifting any relevant information from Felix's medical records. 'That was why he had the shunt put in to redirect cerebral spinal fluid?'

'That's nearly four years ago now. And the only symptoms he had were to do with his eyes. The squint and the blurred vision.'

'It's possible that an obstruction could be causing problems.' Jonno watched Dave fit a cover to a tympanic thermometer. 'What's his temperature?'

'Thirty-seven point eight.'

High enough to suggest an infection but not high enough to cause a febrile convulsion. Jonno was mentally listing other potential causes of a seizure in a paediatric patient, like high or low blood sugar, an electrolyte disturbance like low sodium levels, concussion from a head injury, the ingestion of drugs or the presence of a brain lesion when two things happened.

Simon arrived.

And Felix began having another seizure.

It was Dave who made the call of status epilepticus. 'That's two seizures in a matter of minutes without regaining consciousness in between.' He was opening equipment packs. 'Let's get IV access, but I'd like to get some intranasal midazolam on board stat.'

It was Simon who administered the medication and drew up another dose in case it was needed. Dave set up what he needed to put an IV cannula in when the jerking of Felix's limbs had subsided. Jonno was watching the little boy like a hawk, finding himself having to resist the urge to cradle his head to protect him from any injury from the wooden floorboards. It felt as if Brie was reading his mind when she pulled the jumper she was wearing over her head and folded it to provide a thin pillow. One minute stretched into another but still the seizure continued. Another dose of medication was administered.

Jonno watched the oxygen saturation levels dropping to less than ninety percent before the medication could take effect on the seizure and, when it slowed enough for Dave to find a vein in Felix's hand to slip the needle into and the interference on the monitor screen to settle, Jonno could see that Felix's heart rhythm was abnormal. His lips were becoming an alarmingly dusky shade of blue, as well.

Simon reached for a bag mask unit to try and improve the oxygen levels.

'Oxygen saturation isn't coming back up.' It was Simon that Dave was speaking to. 'Keep bagging him. I'm going to get ready for a rapid sequence intubation in case those levels don't improve in the next couple of minutes.'

'I can do that.' Jonno reached for the airway kit but Dave shook his head.

'Sorry, Jonno. I can't let you do that. You know the rules about invasive procedures on members of your own family.'

His own family…

Shocked, Jonno moved out of the way as Dave and Simon took over managing what was becoming a critical situation for Felix. He found himself closer to Brie. The mother of his child. Did that automatically make *her* a part of his own family too?

In this moment, it certainly felt like it. And he knew how scared she was because he was feeling a good dose of that fear himself, especially when they both had to shuffle back and give Dave and Simon the room they needed to take over control of Felix's airway and breathing. He could cope with watching Dave draw up the medications that would paralyse and sedate a small body, choose a paediatric size of laryngoscope blade and endotracheal tube and even Simon pre-oxygenating Felix before removing the bag mask to allow Dave to position the small head and open his mouth to insert the blade of the laryngoscope.

But then it suddenly became too real. This was a fight to keep Felix breathing. To keep him alive. The start of a journey to find out what had gone wrong in the first place and to provide treatment that would hopefully make sure it wasn't going to happen again. They had no idea right now what was going to happen in the next minutes, hours or days and...

And it was unexpectedly terrifying...

Jonno wasn't sure whether it was him or Brie that stretched out a hand first but it didn't matter. They both needed one to hold and who better to hold it than the other person who was so deeply invested in keeping this child safe.

His fingers felt numb by the time Felix was

successfully intubated and his oxygen levels were steadily rising.

'Let's get him on the stretcher.' Dave nodded. 'I'll come in the ambulance with you and we'll call ahead to let them know we're on our way. Brie, you'll want to come to with us, yes?'

'Please...' Brie let go of Jonno's hand and went to help settle Felix onto the stretcher. 'I'll grab my phone. Mum's at work. She'll want to be with us when we get there.'

Jonno was packing up some of the gear but he could feel the touch of Brie's gaze and he knew what she was thinking but was not about to say aloud.

That his father was Felix's other grandparent.

That he should know what was happening too.

Jonno got into the rapid response vehicle to follow the ambulance. He tapped a contact number in his phone and it came through on Bluetooth as he pulled away from Brie's house.

'St Nicholas Children's Hospital. How may I help you?'

'Could you page Dr Anthony Morgan for me please?' Jonno knew he sounded brusque but this was no time to be hesitant. 'It's urgent.'

'Who's calling, please?'

Jonno took a deep breath. 'Jonathon Morgan. I'm his son.'

That Brie's life had fundamentally changed had never been more obvious than when she found herself watching Dr Peter Jarvis, the head of paediatric neurosurgery at Bristol's St Nicholas Children's Hospital, walk away from the discussion they'd just had, with Jonno Morgan standing beside her and not her mother. For the first time ever, Felix had both his parents involved in any decision-making on his behalf. Two people who could sign the necessary consent forms.

Elsie was in the intensive care unit, through the double doors in the corridor behind them, sitting beside the bed where Felix lay, sedated and on a ventilator, holding her grandson's hand. An operating theatre was on standby for the next step in managing what felt like the worst crisis Brie had faced so far in her son's life and her head was spinning with all the information she was trying, desperately, to retain.

Jonno was watching her. 'Are you okay?'

Brie was fighting tears. 'Not really...' she

admitted. 'I might need a minute before I go back in. I don't want to scare my mum. Or Felix. What if he's aware of what's happening around him at some level?'

'I'm quite sure that he's deeply asleep. The atmosphere around him is different when he has people that love him there, but he's got that right now. His nana obviously adores him. He's probably dreaming about riding that pony he loves so much. What's its name?'

'Bonnie.' Brie's response was more like a strangled sob.

'Come in here for a minute...' Jonno touched her shoulder, guiding her into an empty relatives' space that had comfortable seating, tea and coffee-making facilities and a large-sized box of tissues on a coffee table. 'You can talk to me about anything that's scaring you. Sometimes just talking about it can help to keep you strong. And Felix needs you to be strong.'

The calm encouragement in Jonno's tone, along with the touch on her shoulder, was already helping and Brie knew it could be some time before Felix would be taken to Theatre. She sank onto the edge of a couch cushion and buried her head in her hands to try and gather her strength. 'I forgot to bring a notebook,' she said. 'I'm never going to remember everything Dr Jarvis told us.'

Jonno crouched in front of her. 'You don't have to,' he said gently. 'All those results from the blood tests—the white cell count and the metabolic panel and the blood gas—have ruled out a lot of things. It's clear that Felix is fighting a nasty infection and the most likely cause for that is a shunt infection. That pocket of fluid they found near the end of the shunt on the abdominal ultrasound was the reason Dr Jarvis went ahead with collecting the sample of cerebral spinal fluid from the shunt valve reservoir and, as soon as they get the initial results on that and make sure they've got him started on the best antibiotics, he wants to take him straight to Theatre to remove the shunt.'

Brie nodded. Watching them put a needle under the skin behind Felix's tiny ear to find that cerebral spinal fluid reservoir had been yet another procedure that Brie hadn't expected and could never be really prepared for. Nowhere near as awful as seeing him being intubated at home and then rushed into Emergency but it had been another graphic reminder of how vulnerable her little boy was right now and… Brie was feeling almost that vulnerable herself.

Vulnerable and so very frightened. Maybe Jonno could sense that because she felt his hand rubbing her knee in a gesture of empathy.

'I get why they need to remove the shunt.' Brie's indrawn breath was shaky. 'But I'm not sure I understood what he was saying about administering the antibiotics.'

'If they take out the shunt, they need to put in an external ventricular drain. It's a system that works on gravity to help drain excess cerebral spinal fluid. They can use the same system to deliver intrathecal antibiotics straight into the CSF and monitor the intracranial pressure at the same time. Felix will need to stay in the ICU while that's in place and will have nursing staff with him at all times.'

Brie felt a tear trickle down the side of her nose. 'He's never been this sick before,' she said quietly. 'And he's had so many surgeries already.'

'Even before he was born,' Jonno agreed. 'The reports about that surgery in his folder were just clinical but I remember you talking about it on the beach that day and I can only imagine how hard that must have been for you.' He reached behind him and pulled tissues from the box on the table to press into

Brie's hands. 'And you got through that. Even when you had to travel to another country to have it done. And stay there for weeks and weeks. You're strong, Brie. You're right about him being the best kid in the world but, you know what?' He didn't wait for her response. 'You're the best mum.'

Brie shook her head. 'I've never felt like that. I've just tried to make the best decisions I could.' She swallowed hard, remembering another time she had to struggle to take in everything a medical team were telling her. 'And I didn't do it alone. I couldn't have. Mum was the amazing one. She got a mortgage on her house so we could afford to go to Switzerland and have the surgery. She resigned from her job. She's been with me every step of the way.'

She heard the way Jonno cleared his throat as if it was painful.

'I wish I'd been there,' he said softly. 'I'm sorry you had to go through that as a single parent. I *would* have been here if I'd known...'

'I know...' Brie blew her nose. She did believe that. In a way, it might have been a good thing that she hadn't been able to contact him and tell him about his impending parenthood. He might have come back to Bristol. He might even have thought he needed to 'do the right thing' and offer to marry her so they could raise their child together, but that could well have been a disaster. It hadn't exactly worked out well for his parents, had it?

'I need to go back to Felix and bring Mum up to speed with what's been decided.' But Brie took a moment to take a deep breath to gauge whether she could control her tears. 'What was that other thing that Dr Jarvis mentioned? That he said we could wait and talk about later? After they get on top of this infection?'

'There's a surgery he could have that would mean he doesn't need another shunt put back in, maybe for the rest of his life, so the danger of another infection would be gone. It's called an EVT—an endoscopic third ventriculostomy.'

Brie's brain was refusing to make sense of the words. It was more than she could cope with to think about further brain surgery for Felix.

Jonno must have seen that in her face. 'You don't need to even think about that yet,' he told her. 'One step at a time, okay? You've done it before and you can do it now. We're going to get through this. *All* of us. I know I'm very new at being a father but...you know how much I love Felix, don't you? That I'll do anything I can to protect him?'

It was that wobble in his voice that told Brie he was just as scared as she was. And maybe he'd only known his son for a very short time but she could clearly remember the first time she'd laid eyes on her baby—with that first ultrasound—and she knew how instantly it was possible to fall in love with your child. She knew how much Jonno loved Felix. He was here now and she knew he would be here for his son whenever he was needed from now on.

And then, kneeling on the floor, Jonno wrapped his arms around her in a physical connection unlike anything Brie had ever felt before. The only times before this that she'd been this close to Jonno was when they had been making love. This had absolutely nothing to do with any physical attraction but it was a form of love.

Of caring.

Of sharing. Because Brie knew how much Jonno already loved his son and this had to be just as traumatising for him as it was for her.

So she held him back. Tightly.

So tightly she didn't see someone coming into this space.

'Oh…excuse me…' It was a male voice. 'I didn't mean to interrupt.'

Oh…no…

Jonno let go of Brie and hurriedly got to his feet. He hadn't been anywhere near ready to let go of Brie so his first reaction as he faced his father felt like resentment. She'd needed the comfort of that hug.

He'd needed it.

But, for some unidentifiable reason, he was embarrassed that his father had seen them. Was it because he didn't want Anthony to think there was anything going on between himself and Brie? That he might be considering a relationship with the mother of his son—marriage, even—simply because they shared a child?

As if…

You only had to look at his own family to know what a terrible idea that was.

His resentment was hard to hang onto, however, as he saw how strained his father's face was. How embarrassed he was that he might have interrupted an emotional moment.

'I'm so sorry I couldn't be here any earlier. I was in the middle of a Fontan procedure for a three-year-old with hypoplastic left heart syndrome. It's a complex surgery that I couldn't hand over to anyone else.'

'It's not a problem,' Jonno said. 'It's not as if you could have done anything. I just thought you should know.'

Anthony's nod was slow. 'Thank you.'

Brie was on her feet now. 'I need to get back to Felix. I want to stay with him until he has to go to Theatre.'

'Theatre?' Anthony's eyebrows rose. 'The message I got was that he'd had a seizure.'

'I'll get him up to speed,' Jonno told Brie. 'You go and be with Felix.'

'Thank you.' Brie smiled at Anthony. 'And thank you for coming.'

'If there *is* something I can do, please don't hesitate to ask.' The older man's face was serious but there were crinkles at the corners of his eyes that suggested a smile. 'You know, it's quite extraordinary, but looking at you is like seeing your mother a few decades ago.'

'And you look like an older version of Jonno.' Brie bit her lip. 'Oh…sorry… I shouldn't have said that, should I? When you're not…'

'Jonathon's biological father? It's okay… you're not the first person to say that but DNA doesn't lie.'

Jonno was cringing inside. He'd accused

Brie of lying to him and being just the same as his parents but he was no better, was he?

'I never actually did a DNA test,' he said. 'I just said I did.'

There was a long moment of stunned silence in that small room.

Anthony closed his eyes. 'It was always a possibility,' he said. 'That's why it was so believable.'

'I could do one now. So we'd all know the truth.'

Anthony shook his head. 'It wouldn't make any difference.' He opened his eyes and looked straight at Jonno. His words were quiet and straight from the heart. 'You'll always be my son.'

The emotion in that room was overwhelming. It was Brie who made it bearable.

'And you'll always be Felix's grandpa,' she told Anthony. 'And you know what?'

'What?'

'I've always seen Jonno in Felix. Now I can see where they've both got their Morgan genes from. You've all got the same eyes. Like peas in a pod.'

Brie's own eyes were filling with tears again and Jonno wanted nothing more than to stay close to her and offer her whatever support and reassurance he could. Perhaps he wanted to try and explain why he'd lied to his father all those years ago, but she was already through the door and heading back to the ICU.

He wanted to follow her. So that he too could be near his son before he got wheeled up to Theatre. Instead, he was going to have to sit and talk to his father for the first time in so many years. For the first time since he'd learned he was a father himself. It was getting too close to painful, shut-off places to even think about Anthony saying he would always be his son but the least he could do was to apologise for that lie.

Jonno took a very deep breath.

'I'm sorry, Dad,' he said.

Anthony shrugged. 'It's ancient history,' he said quietly. 'How 'bout you tell me what's going on with *your* son?'

Talking about clinical matters was so much easier. They sat side by side on the couch and Jonno told him everything they had found out so far and what the plan was to treat the infection Felix had somehow picked up.

What he didn't say was how heartbreaking this was. That he'd only just discovered he was a father but he felt as if he was failing in the only responsibility that really mattered, which was to protect his child.

But maybe he didn't need to say anything. It was Anthony who broke the heavy silence when Jonno stopped talking.

'It's never easy,' he said softly. 'Being a parent.'

The silence became even heavier. To his horror, Jonno could feel tears gathering at the back of his eyes. 'How would you know?' he heard himself asking, his voice raw. 'You were never there...'

'I wanted to be. I tried to be. You were the reason I married your mother but that meant she made all the rules in the marriage. I couldn't break them because she had all the power.'

'You didn't break them because you were weak,' Jonno muttered.

'I didn't break them because, if I had, I would have lost my son. Julia would have taken you away and I might never have seen you again and...and I couldn't let that happen.' Anthony's outward breath was a sigh. 'But I ended up losing you anyway. And I couldn't blame you for being so angry.'

'I hated you then,' Jonno admitted. 'But I hated the whole world at that point and, after I'd found a way to escape, I never wanted to go back.'

'I know.' Anthony got to his feet. 'And

I couldn't force you to do anything. Especially when I knew it was quite possible that I wasn't your biological father. Your *real* father...'

Jonno stood up. He was about to open his mouth and apologise again. Maybe to tell him that being a 'real' father was about a lot more than simply biology. But Anthony put his hand up and stopped him speaking.

'You need to be with *your* son right now,' he said. 'We can talk another time.' His smile was tentative. 'I hope...?'

Jonno gave a single nod.

'I might see if Elsie would like a bit of a break.' Anthony turned towards the door. 'I could take her down to the café for a coffee, maybe. And that way, you and Brie can stay with Felix together.'

Jonno led the way back into the ICU but he was very aware of the man following him.

His father.

He was a father himself now. Had Anthony ever felt about him the way he felt about Felix? How would he feel if Brie wanted to control how close he could be to his son? Maybe his father hadn't thought that his work as a famous paediatric surgeon was so much more important than his own family. Maybe giving more and more of himself to that work had been his way of coping with heartbreak. The way that Jonno's passionate involvement in adrenaline sports had been the way he'd learned to cope when emotions got too big?

It was only a short time after Elsie had accepted Anthony's suggestion of going for a coffee that Felix was taken up to Theatre to have his shunt removed. Jonno and Brie followed his bed. They went past the relatives' room and then waited at the lift to go up a floor. They walked the long corridor to the Theatre suite, where they were allowed into the anaesthetic room adjacent to the operating theatre for a minute or two before they had to say goodbye.

Jonno had been holding Brie's hand ever since the journey to Theatre had started. He was still holding it as she bent to smooth a dark tress of hair from Felix's forehead to place a soft kiss on his pale skin.

And he still hadn't let go when they both went back to the relatives' room to wait, because he had the strong feeling that Brie didn't want him to let go.

There wasn't much that he could do, but at least it was something.

CHAPTER TWELVE

THE WAITING WAS the hardest part.

Waiting for Felix to come out of the operating theatre after having his shunt removed. Waiting to see how quickly the pressure inside his skull could return to normal so that he would no longer be at risk of any seizures. Watching the fluid collect in the CFS drainage system that relied on gravity and had valves that had to be carefully closed and then opened again whenever Felix changed his position. Waiting for the antibiotics to get on top of the infection that had made him so sick.

The first twenty-four hours were the worst and there was no way Jonno was about to let Brie and her mother keep vigil alone. He barely left the room himself that first day. Anthony came and went throughout the day and into the evening, between commitments to his patients. Elsie ferried coffee from the café and tried to persuade both Jonno and Brie to take a break and find something to eat much later that evening after the café had closed but Brie wasn't going anywhere.

'I can't,' she said quietly. 'I have to be here when he wakes up.'

'I'll go, then,' Elsie offered. 'I could bring you both back a hamburger or something?'

'I can do that,' Jonno said. 'I might duck back to my apartment and have a quick shower and change out of this uniform. I'll bring food back.' He closed his eyes briefly, as he remembered that it was only a couple of days ago that he and Brie and Felix had been eating hamburgers together after that dance class. That he'd made his son laugh and laugh and laugh by using the longest French fries as walrus tusks. He had to swallow hard to get rid of that lump in his throat. 'Cheeseburger for you, right?' He smiled at Brie. 'With extra bacon?' He turned to Elsie. 'Can I get you something as well?'

Elsie shook her head. 'I'll go home when you get back,' she said. 'I'm going to need a shower myself.'

'You should go home and get some sleep soon, Mum,' Brie said. 'I'm going to be here all night. I'll call you if anything changes.'

Elsie shrugged. 'Maybe…but I'm not going to leave you here by yourself.'

'She won't be by herself,' Jonno said. 'I'll be back very soon and then I won't be going anywhere.'

He met the steady gaze of Brie's mother and held it until he saw some of the deep lines around her eyes and mouth soften a little. Until he knew she'd got the message that he could be trusted.

She was still there when he got back and this time she smiled at him with a warmth that made him remember what his father had said to Brie about how like her mother she looked and he could see it himself now. Elsie Henderson was still a very beautiful woman.

'Go and have your dinner,' she told them. 'I'll hold the fort until you get back and I'll come and get you if Felix wakes up, but I have the feeling he's going to sleep for the rest of the night.'

'His temperature's come down,' Brie told him as they walked to the relatives' room where he'd left the paper bags of hot food outside the ICU. 'So has the intracranial pressure. Dr Jarvis popped in while you were gone and he's happy with how he's doing. Your dad came in too. He's got a post-surgery patient in the unit that he's with at the moment.'

Hamburgers really hadn't been the best choice of food, he decided a few minutes later, when he saw Brie unwrap hers and simply stare at it. And then she picked a French fry from the small cardboard container and her gaze flew up to meet his and he knew she was thinking about the walrus tusks. Jonno could see the moment her eyes filled with tears and how determined she was to blink them away and stay strong.

'What's in the other bag you brought in?'

'My laptop. I thought I could find something to entertain Felix with when he wakes up. And I brought that folder of his medical notes too. I haven't quite finished reading all those school reports.' Jonno put his hamburger down, still wrapped. He wasn't feeling very hungry either. He reached into the carrier bag and pulled out the folder and as he did so an envelope fell out.

'Oops…' He reached down and picked it up. Puzzled, he turned it over in his hand. The envelope was sealed and stamped. It had several date stamps from seven years ago as well as the postage stamp. And it was covered with other stamps of words, only a couple of which were in English. Words like 'Return to Sender' and 'Unknown at this Address'.

The address of the Mount Everest Base Camp, Khumbu, Nepal. With his name above it.

'Oh, my God…' He raised a startled gaze to find Brie. 'You wrote to me? Snail mail?'

Brie was watching him back intently but she didn't say anything. She simply nodded.

Jonno shook his head slowly. 'There are two base camps,' he told her. 'The south camp is in Nepal. The north one is in Tibet, on the opposite side of the mountain.'

Brie's eyes widened. 'I didn't know that. And you were in the north camp?'

It was Jonno's turn to nod. 'Can I…open it?'

She shrugged. 'Not much point now.' She offered him a wry smile. 'It's kind of old news.'

But Jonno opened the envelope anyway. It only took seconds to read but then he took another breath and read it again more slowly.

Dear Jonno,
   I know this will come as a shock, but I have to tell you that I'm pregnant with your baby. I wasn't lying to you when I said I was on the pill, but I was sick

*the next day and something went wrong.
I'm sorry.*

*I'm past my first trimester now. I don't
expect anything from you at all and it's
fine if you don't want any part of this—
I just thought you should know that you
are going to have a child in the world in
about five months' time. A baby that I'm
going to keep and am going to take care
of and love in the very best way I can.*

*I will love him—or her—enough for
both of us and I'll tell them about their
father and how very special he is.*

All the best, Brie.

There was a smudge on the paper below
that line. It could be words that had been
rubbed out. Or tears that had fallen?

PS, she had added. *I will never forget you.
Or that night.*

Brie was watching closely enough to see the
moment that Jonno remembered accusing her
of having lied to him from the moment they'd
met. Not that this letter was proof that she had
been taking an oral contraceptive that night,
but it was certainly proof that she'd done everything she could to contact him when she
knew she was pregnant.

She could see the apology in his eyes.

And she thought she could see him offering her the gift of trust and that was huge, coming from Jonno, when he'd had his ability to trust broken so badly at a time when he had so needed something solid to hang onto in his life.

It *was* huge. But it also felt fragile so Brie didn't want to risk saying anything that might make Jonno take a step back. Instead, she put her uneaten food back in the bag.

'I might go back and see how Felix is doing,' she said quietly. 'Thanks so much for bringing the food, though. I can always heat it up later.'

'I'll come with you.' Jonno's voice sounded rough, which might be why he needed to clear his throat. 'I'm not that hungry myself now.'

They found Anthony in the room with Elsie. 'I'm trying to persuade your mum to go home and get some sleep,' he told Brie. 'But she said the couch in the relatives' room would be good enough.'

'Go home, Mum.' Brie gave her mother a hug. 'I'll call you if anything changes, I promise.'

'Are you okay to drive?' Jonno asked. 'I could call you a taxi.'

'There's no need for that,' Anthony said

firmly. 'I'm heading home myself and I can drop you off, Elsie.'

'Oh...' Elsie blinked. 'In that case...' She turned back to Brie. 'Are you sure you don't want me to stay?'

Brie shook her head. 'We'll be fine,' she said.

And she didn't mean herself and Felix in that 'we'. She meant herself and Jonno— in what felt like a partnership that had just moved into a different space. One that had the beginnings of things that were much more solid than an irresistible physical attraction.

Things like forgiveness. And trust.

Only the following day Felix was sitting up in bed, feeling so much better he was wondering what all the fuss was about. Amazingly, he was far less bemused by the fact that someone he'd only known as a helper at his riding class and as a friend of Mummy's was visiting him so often, but maybe a lifetime of medical support and therapies had brought so many adults into his life on a regular basis it was no big deal. And maybe it was just wishful thinking, but it felt as if there was a real connection there. That Felix already loved his daddy even though he still had no idea who Jonno really was?

There seemed to be an unspoken agreement between Jonno, Brie, Elsie and Anthony that it was time to tell Felix why his family had suddenly doubled in size but, equally, there was a silent pact to wait until he was well enough. Nobody wanted to upset him in any way. They were, in fact, all going out of their way to make him feel as good as possible.

A few days later, when all four adults happened to be visiting at the same time and they decided to go to the café for some coffee because Felix was sound asleep, the consensus was that if there had been a competition going on for who could make Felix feel happiest then Jonno would have won it hands down.

'How did you know,' Elsie asked, 'that his favourite book was the one about that spotty pony Nobby running away to join a circus?'

'He told me. When I had been telling him about riding ponies in the desert. He thought Nobby would like to do that.'

'Why did I never think to try and find out if there was a sequel?' Brie was shaking her head but smiling at the same time. 'Who knew that Nobby would think circus tricks were so silly he didn't want to do them and he'd get sold to a cowboy?'

'And who knew that somebody would be

smart enough to make a Nobby soft toy to sell along with the book?' Elsie's smile was misty. 'Did you see the way he was hanging onto him and using him for a pillow while he's asleep?'

Jonno was embarrassed by the appreciation of his gift. 'I just did a search online,' he said. 'It was no big deal.'

Except it really was, wasn't it? The way Felix's face had lit up. The squeeze of those small arms around Jonno's neck as he'd thanked him had felt as if they were actually tightening around his heart hard enough to take his breath away.

'It's a big deal for Felix,' Brie assured him. Her eyes were thanking him all over again. 'He thinks you're more amazing than Father Christmas.'

'We'll have to make sure Dennis doesn't get hold of Nobby when we get home,' Elsie warned. 'He's got such a talent for eating the ears off any soft toy animals.'

'That might be a wee while yet,' Anthony warned. 'They want to keep a close eye on him and watch for any sign of increasing ICP until he's been clear of the infection long enough to replace the shunt. Or do the EVT?' He looked from Jonno to Brie. 'Has Peter Jarvis talked to you both about that again?'

Brie nodded. 'I was trying to explain it to Mum this afternoon.' Jonno could see the careful way she was taking a deep breath and it made him notice how tired she looked. He'd never seen shadows that deep beneath her eyes. 'I know it would be great if it meant he would never need another shunt but it sounds really scary.'

'It's a well-established, minimally invasive endoscopic procedure now,' Anthony said. 'With promising results. I had a good chat to Peter about it today.'

'I don't really understand it all,' Elsie confessed. 'But deliberately making holes in someone's brain does sound a bit horrific.'

Anthony gave her a quick reassuring smile. 'It's a tiny hole,' he told her. 'And the procedure only takes about thirty minutes. It's called minimally invasive because it's not a major surgery.'

'That's a risk in itself, isn't it?' Brie asked. 'With the hole being so small, it can close up.'

'But the long-term complication rate is lower than it is for shunts,' Jonno put in. 'And I certainly don't want to see him go through another infection in the years to come.'

His own words seemed to catch in the air. Jonno could see that Anthony and Elsie weren't listening because his father was drawing on a paper serviette to explain the procedure of an endoscopic third ventriculostomy more clearly to Elsie but he could also see—or, rather, sense—that Brie had gone very still.

In the years to come…

It would be a rather casual way to be making a public commitment to being involved in his son's life, if that was what he was doing.

Was it?'

Was he making a promise to be here as Felix's father, alongside his mother? Like a real family?

Good grief…they even had an extended family with the grandparents already involved.

It was Jonno's turn to take a deep breath. It wasn't that he didn't trust Brie enough to know that they could make it work. How could he not trust her after finding that letter that proved the lengths she had taken to try and tell him he was going to become a father?

But his own father was back in his life again and that was stirring some big emotions. Memories of how it felt to believe that he'd never been loved as much as he'd desperately wanted to be. Of needing to escape because there was nothing in the world that could really be trusted.

Jonno could feel that need to escape hovering at the back of his mind, fanned by the knowledge that he'd already made a big decision today. Did Brie see that in his face when she caught his gaze? Or had she actually tuned into his thoughts?

'When's the settlement date on your apartment?' she asked.

'Not for another month.' But the clock was already ticking, wasn't it? 'My mate Max is happy for me to crash on his couch for a while but I do need to start looking for another property. Especially since I told the Air Rescue management that I'm happy to sign up for that job.'

He'd been speaking quietly but that didn't stop his words catching their parents' attention. Talking about being involved in the years to come was one thing. Taking on a new career and investing in property was something else. Something that could mean Jonno's involvement in Felix's life—and, by default, in Brie's life, along with her mother and *his* father—was going to be life-changing for them all.

'You're taking the job on the helicopters?' Elsie asked. 'Oh…that's such exciting news.'

'You're looking for property?' Anthony asked.

'I'm selling the apartment,' Jonno told him quietly. 'It's something I should have done a very long time ago. It's time to move on.'

He let his gaze rest on Brie for a heart-beat, hoping that she would understand that there were some memories associated with that apartment that he didn't necessarily want to move on from? Memories that were theirs and theirs alone? It took only another beat of time to know that the message had been received. Even better, that Brie wasn't about to forget them either. She'd already told him that, hadn't she? In that postscript in her letter.

I will never forget you. Or that night...

Thank goodness nobody else was picking up on any intimate silent communication.

'It's time I downsized,' Anthony said. 'I'd like something about the size of your place, Elsie. That garden of mine is taking up far too much time to maintain and I barely use most of the rooms in the house. I've only kept it because I grew up there myself.' He reached for his coffee cup to finish his drink, but then replaced it carefully on its saucer as he caught his son's gaze.

'It's where *you* grew up,' he said softly.

'It's as much your home as mine, Jonno. You should have a say in whether it gets sold or not. Maybe you'd like to live there again yourself? Felix would love the garden, wouldn't he?'

Jonno had told Brie that the house had been a perfect place to grow up in, with the nearby forest park and bike trails, but in reality his life had been a long way from perfect. Would it be a huge mistake to revisit the past to that extent, in the hope that history could be rewritten?

'Thanks,' he said to his father. 'It's certainly something to think about.'

But his tone was dismissive and an awkward silence fell that seemed to be overflowing with things that maybe both father and son wanted—or needed—to talk about but neither of them had any idea how to start, or if they even *should* start. Jonno was aware of a sensation as if there were walls closing in around him. Of being trapped...?

Elsie was the first to respond to the tension. She got to her feet. 'I'll head back upstairs,' she announced. 'I'm sure Felix is still sound asleep but I'd like to tidy up his toys before I go home tonight.'

'I'd better get moving too.' Anthony was clearly relieved by the escape route Elsie had engineered. 'I've got some patients I need to see before *I* head home.'

A new silence between Jonno and Brie when they were alone, but before Brie could think of a way to break it there was a buzzing sound from his phone lying on the table beside his coffee cup. He silenced the vibration.

'It's just Max,' he said to Brie. 'I'll call him back later.'

But his phone buzzed again against the tabletop and Jonno grimaced as he must have guessed why his friend needed to talk to him so urgently. 'Oh, *no...*'

'What is it?' Brie asked.

'That trip we planned to the Cairngorms to do that rock climbing we missed out on last time, thanks to getting involved with that rescue?'

'I remember. The climb with that odd name. Squareface?'

'That's the one. Fancy you remembering that.'

Jonno sounded impressed, but how could she ever forget when it had been such a part of all of this? Jonno's trip away had given Brie the time and courage to decide she had to tell him about Felix, only to be so thoroughly distracted when she'd arrived at his apartment.

That photo of him and Max in the newspaper, which had been how Elsie had found out Anthony was Felix's grandfather. Jonno finding out he was Felix's father, thanks to that meeting Elsie had arranged.

Jonno's tone was almost a groan. 'It's this week. The day after tomorrow, in fact. I'd been planning to get in touch with him to talk about that trip, but that was the day Felix got sick and it totally fell out of my head.' He picked up his phone. 'I'll call him back. I'll have to cancel it now.'

Brie watched him pick up his phone again, a cascade of thoughts flashing through her head, following on from the series of events that had happened since his last trip to the Cairngorm mountains in Scotland.

She thought of that gleam in his eyes when he'd been talking about how much he would love to try one of those wingsuits that could make you feel as if you were flying. How disappointed he'd been not to get the chance of facing the challenge of that 'gnarly' rock face he and Max had wanted to climb.

She wondered if he was planning to cancel every adventure he might have dreamed of doing in the years to come. The years to come that he was planning to spend helping to keep his son safe and loved as he grew up. Did that go some way towards explaining the tension she'd felt when his father had suggested he went back to living in the house he'd grown up in? A tension that had suggested old wounds were being exposed. That Jonno felt a need to escape? Did he need some time to clear his head—the way she had needed it that first time he'd gone away for a few days with his best mate, to do something they were both passionate about?

Without thinking, Brie put her hand on Jonno's arm to stop him picking up his phone.

'Wait...' she said.

Jonno looked up. 'What is it?'

'It's something Mum said to me a long time ago, when it felt like it might be impossible for us both to be able to combine looking after Felix with other things in life we both wanted to do. Like me becoming a paramedic and Mum going back to her nursing.'

Jonno looked puzzled. He obviously couldn't see how this related to him calling Max.

'She said that if we wanted to be the best parent and grandparent we could be, we have to look after ourselves too. We have to be able to do things that we're passionate about.'

'Your mum is a wise woman.'

'So you'll go? Have some fun doing the kind of stuff you love so much?'

But Jonno looked torn. 'I can't. Not while Felix is in hospital.' His gaze on Brie was intense. 'This has made me realise how much you've had to go through by yourself. It's not going to be like that from now on, Brie. I'm going to be here too.'

In the years to come…

Hearing Jonno say aloud that he was planning to be involved in his son's care in the future was one thing. Taking on a new career and investing in property was even more significant. Jonno's presence in Felix's life— and, by default, in Brie's life—was going to be life-changing for them all.

But…how perfect would it be to be hearing those words because he wanted to be here for *her* and not only to support her in caring for their child? Brie wasn't about to let a flash of heartbreak cloud the significance of the promise Jonno was making, however. And she didn't want to push him away by making it obvious how much more she was longing for, so she kept her tone light.

'He's happy. Thanks to you, he's got Nobby. And a new story we'll probably have to read until we all know it by heart and everyone other than Felix will be sick to death of it.' Brie smiled. 'You'll be back by the time he has to go to Theatre again. And didn't you say that if you didn't go now the weather would get too bad and it might be ages before you got another chance?'

'That's true.' Jonno was holding her gaze. 'Are you sure you don't mind?'

Brie's heart was being squeezed so hard it hurt. Jonno had been prepared to give up something he loved that much for Felix. This was a gift that only she could give him, wasn't it?

'I'm sure,' she said softly. 'Go… Enjoy…'

It wasn't just Brie who missed Jonno being around.

'Where's Jonno?' Felix asked yet again, as Brie tried to settle him for the night.

'He's away, just for a few days,' Brie told him. 'And when he's back he'll be able to tell you all about his exciting adventures climbing mountains. Do you want to look at some pictures of people climbing mountains on your tablet?'

But Felix shook his head. Very uncharacteristically, he even stuck out his bottom lip. 'I want him to read me the story about Nobby and the cowboys.'

'We might be able to find a picture of exactly where Jonno's gone, in the Cairngorms in Scotland. Did he tell you he was going to climb part of a mountain that's got a funny name? A big rock called Squareface?'

Felix still looked mutinous.

Brie sighed. 'Okay... I'll read you the story about Nobby and the cowboys.'

Felix pulled the spotted soft toy horse into his arms as he snuggled down on his pillows. His sigh was even louder than Brie's. 'We're ready, Mumma...'

She had to read the story three times but, while Felix was looking a lot sleepier, he still wasn't looking happy.

'I want to go home,' he said sadly.

'I know.' Brie ruffled his hair and bent down to kiss him. 'It won't be long. Dr Jarvis said we're going to do some more tests and then you might be ready for the operation that will fix things so we can all go home. You and me *and* Nobby.'

But Felix didn't smile back.

'I want to go home now. I want to see my stars and make a wish.'

Brie could see his eyes filling with tears and it was so unlike Felix that her heart broke a little. She picked up his tablet. 'How 'bout I find a picture of some stars?'

'Okay...'

'*Star light, star bright, first stars I see tonight...*' Felix showed little enthusiasm for the rhyme but he closed his eyes tightly as they finished.

'What did you wish for?' Brie asked.

'Same as last time.'

'The special wish?'

'Yeah...' Felix was drifting into sleep, his cheek buried in Nobby's soft neck.

'What was it?'

'Can't tell you or it might not come true...' his voice was getting the familiar slur that told Brie he was barely conscious now '...and then Jonno will never be my daddy...'

Oh...

Brie needed some air. She walked out of Felix's room and down the main corridor of the ward. As she went through the main doors to where a group of comfortable chairs had been placed in front of the windows opposite the lifts, a set of steel doors slid open.

Elsie walked out of the lift.

'Mum...' Brie could feel the blood draining from her face. 'What's wrong? Has something happened to Dennis?'

'No...he's fine. He had a lovely walk. It's something else...' Elsie was right in front of Brie now. 'You'd better sit down, love...'

But Brie couldn't move. 'Tell me...'

'I just heard it on the radio in the car. There's...there's been an accident...'

She knew. Even before Elsie said anything else, Brie knew what had happened. That her worst fear had come to pass.

'They're not giving out any details yet. They just said that a climber's been killed in the Cairngorms. On a peak the locals call Squareface... Oh, love... I'm so sorry...' Elsie's arms were around Brie. 'It might not be Jonno. We can't assume the worst.'

Except that it was impossible not to.

Somehow Brie made it to one of the chairs near the window. She sank onto the edge of it but couldn't find any words. She just stared straight ahead, too stunned to even process what was happening.

'I tried to call Anthony,' Elsie said. 'If it is Jonno, they would have told him first, I'm sure. But I think his phone's switched off, which isn't a good sign, is it?'

'Anthony was here a while back.' Brie's voice was toneless. 'He had to take a patient back to Theatre for some reason, but he didn't think it was going to take too long. If he's finished, you might be able to find him in the ICU.'

Elsie shook her head. 'I can't leave you.'

'I'm okay. I think I need a few minutes by myself, to be honest, Mum. I can't seem to get my head around this.'

'I know…' Elsie had tears running down her cheeks. 'I can't believe it. And the first thing I thought was that you'd been right all along…'

Her words made no sense. 'About what?'

'About not telling Felix. About how awful it would be for him to find out he has a daddy, only to have him disappear.'

Brie found herself fighting to take a breath as her chest tightened painfully. 'You go, Mum. See if you can find Anthony and then we can be sure about what's really happened.'

Except that, deep down, Brie *was* sure.

The worst *had* happened. Brie had lost Jonno and she'd never even told him how much she loved him.

Felix had lost his father before he'd even known he had him.

What seemed even more heartbreaking was that her precious son had a wish—a special wish—that was never going to come true.

CHAPTER THIRTEEN

SHE LOOKED AS though she'd been sitting there
for ever.

Frozen.

Head down and eyes closed as if she was
dealing with a very private, very painful battle.

Dear Lord... Had she heard the news already? The police had informed him that no
names would be released until members of
the family had been told, but that might have
only made it worse. He'd tried to call his father but had only been able to leave a voice
message. Did Brie think that *he* was the one
who had died? Surely he didn't matter so
much to her that she would look as though
the world had ended?

Or did he...?

The mix of overwhelming strong emotions
like grief and fear and...hope...only made it

harder to know what to do in this moment so as not to give Brie a horrible fright.

So he called her name. So softly, it was a whisper he could barely hear himself.

'Brie…?'

She heard him. She looked up and shock was written all over her face as she stumbled to her feet, which was hardly a surprise. He knew he looked terrible. He was still in his climbing gear and there were bloodstains on his clothes. He had what felt like dried dirt or blood on his face and he hadn't even thought to try combing his hair because he'd been too desperate to get here.

To do *this*…

To hold Brie in his arms and let his cheek rest against her hair. To feel her heart beating against his chest and her warmth that he'd known was the only thing that could thaw the ice in his chest. And it did…

Jonno could feel it starting to melt, with trickles of pain that cut like knives as tears rolled down his face.

Brie was crying too. But she'd never even met Max.

'I thought it was you,' she whispered. 'Oh, God, Jonno. I thought I'd lost you for ever.'

He could feel her shaking in his arms,

which made him hold her even more tightly. He'd felt this shattered when he'd been holding his best friend's body in his arms after that fall. When he'd travelled with him on the long journey to bring him back to Bristol, to where his family would be waiting for him.

A journey during which Jonno had realised there was only one person who could help him get through his world falling apart for the second time in his life.

One person he could trust enough to let her hold his heart—if he was brave enough to give it into her care.

If she wanted it…

There had only been one way to find out. One that had brought him here with such urgency he hadn't even bothered to comb his hair or wash his face. And he'd known that, even if Brie didn't feel the same way, he had to tell her.

Because life was so horribly fragile and you never knew what might be around the next corner. Brie deserved to know how special she was.

How much he loved her…

And Felix had to know that he had a daddy who loved him with all his heart. A heart that might be hurting unbearably right now, but that wasn't simply because it had lost something precious. It was because it was getting bigger. Cracking open. And yeah, that meant that it was open to pain, but it also meant it was open to the opposite of pain.

To the warmth and light and pure joy that love could bring in the good times.

And the comfort and support and hope it could bestow in the not so good times.

So Jonno held Brie even more closely in his arms, just for a heartbeat, because he knew he would have to let her go so that she could take a breath very soon.

'I love you,' he whispered, right against her ear. 'I love you, Brie…'

She felt his arms loosen, which was a good thing because she really needed to take a breath. But the last thing she wanted was for Jonno to let her go.

Ever…

Free enough to tip her head back, Brie looked up at the man she loved so much and her heart hurt for him because he looked so shattered.

There was happiness there as well, though. Sheer relief that he had not only survived some terrible accident that had claimed his best friend, but that he had chosen to come and find her to hold and be held.

Pure joy that he'd said those three, totally life-changing words and she'd known he'd meant every one of them with his whole heart.

It was her turn now. She reached up to touch his face and smooth away some of those tears.

'I love you, Jonno,' she whispered back. 'I always have.' She had to sniff and brush away tears on her own face. 'I could see you in our boy and I've missed you being in our lives, even though you never had been, and... and while I've been sitting here, thinking the worst, I realised that I always *will* love you and I hated that I hadn't told you that. I hated that we'd waited to tell Felix the truth.'

'We don't have to wait any longer, do we?' Jonno pulled her back into his arms. 'From now on, we need to make the most of every minute we can be together as a family.'

Brie tightened her arms around him. 'We might need to wait just a little bit longer,' she said. Not that she was going to tell him he might give Felix a fright if he went in looking like he'd fallen off a mountain himself.

Jonno was nodding agreement but he seemed to be giving her words a very different meaning because he bent his head to touch her lips with his own. Softly. Slowly...

She should take him home, Brie thought. He needed a shower and a change of clothes. It would be good if she could persuade him to eat something, but what he needed most of all was comfort.

Love...

There would be time for everything else after that. They had the rest of their lives to work out how to become the best family they could possibly be. Brie heard the lift doors sliding open behind her and turned her head to see Anthony and Elsie walking out towards them. She could see an oddly similar expression on their faces and she understood exactly why. They were parents and they were both looking at their children with the kind of love that clearly didn't diminish over so many years.

'Oh, thank goodness...' Elsie was smiling through her tears. 'Anthony had already got your message, Jonno. We were coming down to tell Brie but...'

'I think we might be interrupting, Elsie,' Anthony said. 'Shall we go and check on Felix instead?'

'We were just going to do that,' Brie heard herself saying.

Elsie knew what she was saying. Her eyes widened. 'We'll go and get some fresh air,' she said. 'Maybe a coffee. We can come back later.' She gave Anthony a look that made him blink and start following her instantly.

Jonno's eyebrows were raised and he put his hand to his hair as if he'd just remembered how messy it was. 'He won't want to see me like this.'

But Brie smiled. That didn't really matter, did it? Jonno could give his face a quick wash and put a gown over his clothes but Felix would probably only see his daddy's smile, anyway. And the look in his eyes when he found out that both his parents loved not only him but each other... That they were going to become a family.

'He wants to see you more than anything.' Brie took Jonno's hand in hers. 'You have just been given a magic power to make a little boy's wish come true.'

'I hope that's true.'

'I promise you it is.'

Jonno pulled her closer. They were alone in the foyer again and Brie knew he wanted to hold her again for a moment before they went in to see their son. Maybe he wanted to give her another one of those oh, so tender kisses.

And that was fine by her.

Because it wasn't just Felix's wish that was coming true...

* * * * *